DO

(A Colourful Life)

Tony Kearns

INCUNABULA

DOOKIE
A Colourful Life

First published by **Incunabula** 2023

Copyright © **Tony Kearns**

cover artwork by **Jacques Dingue**

www.incunabulamedia.com

ISBN 978-1-4477-5535-7

DOOBIE

Part 1

BEHIND ENEMY LINES

It's graduation day for our hero Dookie, and the guys. They are now fully fledged fighting machines. They've spent sixteen weeks getting the shit kicked out of them every day by the relentless drill instructors on Corps Island. They aren't the young, hyperactive morons they were! They've been reprogrammed! How to speak, brush their teeth, sleep, eat, dress, stand, sit, shit, shave, wash, climb, push up, pullup, walk, run, punch, kick, stab, shoot, break bones and most importantly... Respect.

Without respect for yourself, (they're taught), you cannot respect anything or anyone else. That's why Dookie had travelled west and joined the Corps! He was a chunky hot head running amuck back in Dragon Valley. Going to get himself flatlined or worse if he didn't learn how to be... Just be himself. The hardest training for the hardest case he figured seems to have paid off. Boot camp and combat training were like Disneyland for the young hyperactive pain in the ass that he had become over the past few years. Such a pain in the ass! That's why he earned the name Dookie. Whilst still a young teenager he had been such a pain to teachers, family, and friends alike, that they all went to Dragon Valley Deed poll offices and got his name changed to Dookie. So, like Madonna and Prince he became a one named wonder. He continued to be a hyperactive pain in the rectum for everyone until he left Dragon Valley for Corps Island.

So, our hero isn't a chunky monkey anymore! And all the physical activity has calmed him down mentally too. Although he hasn't had time to really notice yet, what with all the shouting, running and marching that they managed to squeeze in between the brutal 'Intense Training', Otherwise known as I.T. which usually took place in a large and uneven sand pit. The D.I. would shout an exercise command and the recruits would thrust themselves into the position and in unison begin to rep out. However, those pesky D.I. 's would rarely let them get even one rep out before making them spin around or flip over or jump back up etc. into the next position. All the while getting more covered in sand and sweat and more sand. Oh, what fun they had. This would usually go on until one of the weaker recruits threw up or at least dry heaved a bit.

Now ripped to shreds and calm as fuck, Dookie and his Company of graduating Warriors would be split up and sent straight to the frontlines. Dookie, Baron, Rusty and Joey all have orders to the Southern front as part of India Company. As team Leader, Dookie will lead their squad of four. They are all nervous as hell, but clutch at their weapons, their only true best pals now.

The Graduates are transported on unmarked busses with blacked out windows from the Boot Camp training grounds to the nearby airfield. There they board a large, dark green liner already half full of young fresh-faced Warriors. They are quickly ushered to seats, and all sit down and get strapped in, and the flight takes off to the skies within seconds. No safety display, drinks trolley or in-flight entertainment on this airline! With the relative silence of the first few hours of a tense flight behind them, the silence of the young Warriors is getting to Dookie, and the build-up of tension is, in turn, getting to his guts. They start to bubble and twitch, so he leans forward in his seat; placing his rifle between his legs he begins to bear down on the barrel. Arching the bottom of his back forward as his ass slides back on the seat.

Rusty looks up and sees the contorting Dookie. He yells out at the top of his voice so the whole transport can hear.

"AIR BISCUIT"

As everyone looks up and toward the four buddies at the back of the plane, Dookie's flatch protrudes from his stool cupboard and claps its way loudly, through his tense cheeks and whistles its way out the top of his Cammy trousers. A short silence is observed by the young Warriors, and then, well… The tense silence is now truly broken. The transport of Warriors laughs and howls at the stink bomb as the smelly air biscuit circulates around the cabin like a beach ball blowing its way around on a stormy beach. The rest of the flight is a disaster on Warrior Corps terms. The entire shipment of Warriors is now laughing, joking, and generally pissing around.

Dookie leans into his three buddies and says, "Remember this guys. When it gets dark, remember this. This is the light to walk towards. Happy times. Our time."

Pleased with the happy mess he has created, and his ass for that matter, our hero slopes off to dump one before the jump.

A good hour and three courtesy flushes have gone by, before the ripped but bulky brute succumbs to the pins and needles in his legs. He reluctantly wipes and gingerly stands aloft of his temporary throne. The blood rushes back down to his numb feet and he gives his toes a little wiggle. Turns, flushes one last time, washes his hands and makes it back to his seat.

The company Sgt Major bellows out loud to the still ruckus Warriors, "Packs on India Company, we jump in five minutes."

The newly formed India Company Warriors settles down and get their shit together. Packs on, rifles locked and loaded, and helmets securely strapped on. Dookie and his squad prepare for their first night of warfare. The lights in the transport go off and the first buzzer sounds. The Warriors stand up and hook their cords to the jump line as the rear of the plane opens to reveal the noisy, cold and damp air of the southern border lands. The artillery rounds from the enemy below are nothing more than a pop and a flash like a firework, even to the new Warriors. The second buzzer goes and the red lights at the open rear of the plane flash.

"JUMP! JUMP! JUMP! GO! GO! GO!" calls out the Sgt. Major.

Dookie and his small squad are first off. They run down the causeway and float out and down into the darkness. The plane load of leather neck's follows suit. Guided by the light coming from a small battery of cannons still shooting at the aircraft above, Dookie and his squad pull at the guidance ropes to steer their shoots right at them. Rotating around the area slowly as they fall back to terra firma. Baron slides in first and releases his shoot to the wind. He drops straight to prone with his rifle out, supported by his left elbow and butted into his right shoulder, his eyes wide ready for contact as the squad matches his position one by one.

Dookie gets on the comms to his squad, "Right then guys, our mission is to take these cannons out asap yeah. Should only be about fifteen enemy working them so let's get them secured quickly."

The squad moves into the dimly lit area of the enemy lair. They pause at the outskirts as it's the first time they've seen the enemy. Scruffy, dirty, and ill equipped for battle, they seem, to Dookie and his squad, hungrier and more scared than the mean and scary scum they had been told about.

==

Enemy fighters - the highlights:
These aren't soldiers. They just have nowhere else to be. Most have

walked in human caravans from the cold empty southern wastelands that are ruled by oppressive dictators. They are just looking for a better life. Tales of the free north had spurred them on in the plight to reach for freedom. Yet the north doesn't want them. The days of a free North and East to which Dookie and his squad were born into are gone, but they don't even know it yet.

===

Dookie's squad

Baron:
A nice guy but was raised in a cult for the first fifteen years of his life. Although he escaped, he still believes magic men once wandered the earth. He has since joined a 'faith club', unfortunately he doesn't realise the cult he escaped from fund the club.

Tale of the tape:
Height: 5'8"
Penis name: marriage first please!
Hobbies: Shooting his twelve gauge.

===

Rusty:
This know-it-all has his very own messiah complex and was therefore ejected from the cult that baron escaped from. He kept trying to respond to everyone's prayers, but not everyone prayed for death though. He joined the corps so he could kill at will and be treated like a god by anyone who's not a Warrior Dog.

Tale of the Tape:
5'11"

Penis Name: shroomy
Hobbies: Flower pressing

===

Joey:
just a nice guy. A former paramedic that got sick of dealing with
piss heads and junkies all the time so joined up to see if he could make
a difference in the world.
Tale of the tape:
6'1"
Penis name: It hasn't got one cuz' he's just a normal bloke you
freak!
Hobbies: watching t.v.

===

Our hero steps forward toward the enemy and then pauses for a moment. His squad waits on his next move. But something's not right to our squad leader. He looks around and takes note of the ancient artillery guns, only one enemy fighter has a rifle, and none are in uniforms. This isn't the terrifying enemy they were told about. Shit, he could see in the distance a couple of makeshift tents with women and children sitting around a small fire. With his conscience tingling he lowers his weapon and tells his squad to take a knee. He walks calmly forward and announces himself in a friendly manner.

"Hi guys, I'm Dookie. Can we talk for a minute?"

The opposition pauses. They stop firing the cannons and seemingly all wait for Dookie's next move. He steps toward an old set of garden furniture, pulls a seat out and rests his behind into the old plastic base. He rests his rifle on the table and waves out his right hand as to beckon them to join him. The young southerners look around at one another, whispering back and forth. Then, finally one steps forward and sits at the table across from Dookie.

The young enemy fighter tells Dookie of their plight for a better life and how they have been stopped by 'GreenBacks' from going any further north. Dookie sits and listens and then starts to chuckle.

"Do you really think I'm gonna believe that bullshit dude? GreenBacks are a scary story northern kids are told on camping trips as they are growing up."

The enemy looks stunned, then says he can show Dookie a GreenBack! He jumps up and walks over to a mounted telescope. He repositions it from the sky to just north of their position and zooms in. He signals for Dookie to match him at the telescope. Dookie slowly gets up and goes for a look. As he peers down the lens, he can't believe what he sees, It's an actual GreenBack!! There are loads of them. Surrounded by members of the armed forces from the north; and the Green Backs seem to be in charge. Barking their orders as they were, at the Northern Army General's.

Dookie beckons his squad in to show them. As they each take turns looking down the lens, they stand stunned for some time. The squad now know they've been lied to, and the GreenBacks are real. Which means the stories of their power plays, money hoarding, violence and oppression must also be true too. The squad sit around the little table to discuss for a short while.

After they gather themselves and talk it over and much to the delight of their 'enemy', they agree that the Green Backs need investigating!

The young Warriors, not much for hanging around or

mincing their words, tell their new southern buddies to stop firing the cannons and retarget the GreenBacks' Head Quarters, switch all the lights off, put the fires out and wait for Dookie's signal, just in case they need back up. The squad quickly moves off into the brush and wade across the little river that seems to be the line drawn in the dirt for this war. Dookie and the squad jump from one small tree to another and get straight up to the area where they saw the GreenBacks barking orders at military Commanders. They sneak up and huddle behind a few little bushes just outside the wire fenced compound for a closer look.

From there they can not only see them, but they can hear the GreenBacks pulling the strings of the great northern army. It's clear to the squad that these GreenBacks really dislike the southerners from what they can hear. They don't want them filling up their mostly uninhabited country for sure. Rusty whips his tool out and hacks into their phone lines so he can listen in. After just a few hours, he relays information that they seem to have agreements with a southern leader to keep his brutal regime in place, and therefore keeping his Citizens as the work horses for the north's cheap imported products.

"Fuckers", the squad all mouth to each other.

Dookie gets on the comms to his team to talk to them properly.

"We're sent out here to die for these lying cheating bastards! No way! We're recording as usual so let's copy it all up to the rest of the Corps Warriors and turn this fight around, eh?"

The squad knows this is it for them. They would be branded traitors and hunted like animals. But right is right and wrong is wrong, and the young men can't respect greed and abuse of power like this. So, Rusty sends the files across to all Corps Warriors so they can make their own choices. Meanwhile,

Dookie signals to their new southern buddies to fire their cannons at the compound, and the squad moves back into the river and waits for the mortars to rain down.

A few minutes go by, and the first whistle of a bomb overhead comes in low and fast. Followed by another and another. Direct hit after direct hit. The compound is decimated, smoke billowing from the buildings and vehicles. Dookie and the squad crawl back up the riverbank to mop up any more of those GreenBack twats. They open fire at any moving green object. The GreenBacks are caught totally off guard as the raging squad cuts through the initial survivors with ease. The command centre is taken within minutes. Then Dookie stands on top of the rubble and switches his radio to open comms so all in the area can hear him.

"GreenBacks don't control us god damn it, put your weapons down and leave these poor souls better themselves. The lies stop here."

The remaining GreenBacks and their loyal soldiers retreat with haste. Fearful of Dookie's radio broadcast to his brethren. Those GreenBack bitches aren't waiting around to see which side the Warriors take. And watching the rich, power-hungry control freaks jump in their trucks and helicopters, the Warriors of India Company all sling their weapons to the shoulder and congregate at the command centre. The southerners down their weapons and wade across the river to a new beginning.

EYE FOR AN EYE

As morning breaks, the military units and the southerners are all off in the distance making their way home or to find a new home, finally. Dookie and his small Company of Corps Warriors, now fifty strong, stay put. They know it isn't over for them yet.

As they cook up some beans on the fire for breakfast a message comes down the radio.

"Cpl Dookie. Survivors of India Company. We know who you are. We will break you. You are now disavowed. Cpl Dookie, we have your boy. Out."

The radio goes dead, and the Warriors stand firm. Dookie is raised to his knees. As he reaches for his rifle, Joey grabs it off the table, stands to his feet next to his buddy and proclaims he will remain at Dookie's side until the boy is returned. The Warriors cheer and raise their bean filled spoons to note their solidarity. Dookie returns to his feet slowly. Then looks around at his fellow rabid Warriors. He nods his head slowly down, to accept their help and proclaims.

"I just want the boy back safe. The spoils are yours. Now let's go fuck some shit up"

The Company of newly appointed mercenaries eat up and make their way north to track and trace the young stolen lad.

The Warriors now follow Dookie as some kind of leader, not that he feels it. But as they start out, he has them space out at fifteen-foot intervals and alternate their weapons left hand then right hand going down the line. The company keeps a steely eye out, ready for a GreenBack ambush at any time.

For weeks they follow a steady north march headed straight for the location of the radio signal from that GreenBack kidnapping fuck-knuckle. They march on, carrying their precious ammo and hunting for their food. Weaving through small forest areas and grasslands to keep food plentiful. After weeks of walking, they hit the mountain range at the edge of the uninhabited land. Finally.

One of the guys knows these mountains.

===

Gunner;
A warrant officer with twenty years in service. He grew up on the other side of the range on the lower slopes but went hunting and fishing for weeks on end with his old man all around these mountains.

===

The company follows Gunner through the maze of small cannons and up the rounding mountain. After days of scrambling up the shingled slopes, and climbing through driving wind and rain, they finally reach the top. Gunner tells the tired mercenaries the best way down is to take the nearby river. He reckons he and his dad hollowed out tree trunks in the past to get back home quicker, but it's not like Warriors have axes. How are they gonna cut trees down?

Dookie steps back in and says he has an idea. He winks at Baron and looks down the line of men. Baron laughs and comes to stand with his pal. They look at one another and then point, as if to call out for two of the men, Pete, and Rees. These two carry the big guns! Baron tells them to load up their squad automatic weapons and plough the shit out of a section of forest.

"Oh... well... erm I guess that's one way of doing it guys."

says Gunner.

Dookie and Baron stroll off laughing like naughty children and celebrate the job well done with a freshly cooked squirrel kebab each. The two chuckling morons grab a couple of their fellow mercenaries and our hero shouts to Gunner, "You got this dude; we'll go hunt dinner."

Pete and Rees lock in new belts of ammo, and indeed plough the shit out of about thirty big trees and as many small ones. As per Gunners say so. Gunner, a bit of an eco-Warrior in his time off, wipes his sad little eyes and gets the company to strip the leaves and branches off the trunks with their bayonets. As they do so, the hungry warriors collect all the dead and dying little animals as a nice little snacky snack to cook over the fire, to keep them going 'til dinner.

The hillbillies amongst the company, surmise that maybe logging would be a good career move when all this mercenary work is done. What with the killing of trees, wildlife and the feeling of displacing the ones that survived as a bonus, those loggers must be really happy with themselves?

Gunner has the Warriors group the murdered trees by size. He then splits them off into groups, about ten guys each with three big logs.

The Warriors then begin to weave any ropes and bendy branches between the big logs and place the small logs across them horizontally. They lash them together into makeshift rafts and by the time the sun is beginning to set they have five rafts and fifty makeshift paddles. They move the rafts into position by the riverbank just as the hunting party returns.

The boys bring a feast. Two wild boars, a bunch of fish from the river and some apples and berries. The mercenaries all sit around the campfire munching away for some time. As the night draws in, our hero places Firewatch duties at the edge of camp, each on two-hour posts and everyone else huddles up for warmth in the cool mountain air for a good night's sleep.

As the first light of day breaks on to the idyllic riverbank (except for the large hole in the woodland where the lovely trees once stood), the Warriors wake from yet another hard earned nights sleep and slide the rafts into the cold river water. With some pushing and shoving and a lot of swearing, the lads eventually manage to get loaded up. Certainly, with some soggy bottoms, if nothing else, they begin to paddle slowly down stream. Wet or not, they were all thankful not to be walking again.

They paddle downstream for days on the lazy river, some fishing as they go, some with weapons ready, as they pass through high canyons and then dense forest, with branches and bushes hanging right over the river in places. They make dock where they can each night to dry off, rest and eat the day's catch.

After what has been, to the guys, a nice lazy week on the river, they finally get to the other side of the mountain range, and can see across a vast open landscape of a dirty desert. They spend one last night by the ever-decreasing river to dry off and clean their weapons, before hiking down into the miserable, hot and sandy desert.

Down a small hunting trail that passes through small wooded areas and big boulders alike, the men descend the last few thousand feet at a giddy pace.

They make their way into what they know, from reputation, to be an area of nomads, cast out from areas controlled by (what they now know to be) GreenBacks in the coastal basin area. The basin lies just below the desert drop off, marked by a lawless town of lights they can just make out on the horizon as they close in on it each evening. The radio signal seems to have come from just below the town of lights at the foot of the cliff.

Our hero spends the next few days walking through the desert brushland, telling his crew of Warriors to make friends with these nomads. He assures his company they will be good people, just scared and trying to survive. Dookie also knows they're going to need the Nomads help, if the stories are true of this nameless place, they will hate the GreenBacks too. And he's counting on it!

As they approach the outskirts of the town, Dookie orders them to rest in the bushy desert for the night. He reminds his men it's better to approach in daylight in a place like this.

Morning breaks and Dookie and most of the guys head off. They leave the rifles, S.A.W's and rocket launchers with a squad of ten, camo'd up in the bushes, just in case it all goes tits up. They enter the town from the east, just in front of the rising sun and by the main dirt road. As they walk down the high street, they pool the cash they have on them to buy some cheap food and drinks at a diner.

The Warriors find a nice but cheap eatery, 'Danny's', and fill the place with their sweaty, dirty, smelly arses. They order a shitload of pancakes and coffee and apologize to the wait staff for the smell.

Dookie waits for an approach. "In a town like this, they're gonna come to us." he tells the guys quietly.

True to form, by the time the pancakes arrive a rough-as-fuck toothless git appears at the table. He demands that the leader must go with him to see the town's boss. But Dookie's nobody's bitch. He finishes his pancakes and coffee and tells the boys to relax there for a while. He stands his bulk to his feet and tells the awaiting git to lead the way.

The git rushes down the dirt road to the only two-storey building in town, and impatiently waits at the door as Dookie strolls along behind. The bloated brute should've stopped at four pancakes! As he slowly waddles his swollen belly up to the door, the git tries to hurry him up, but Dookie burps a thunderous smelly burp into his face, leans upon the door frame and rubs his gut.

"Oooh that's better," Dookie states.

The git vomits over his own shoes, just a little, from the natural gag reflex. After all, Dookie's eaten nothing but meat for weeks and weeks and hasn't even thought about brushing his teeth! Once he recomposes himself the git leads the chuckling Warrior to his boss. Up the stairs and through a set of double doors.

A large old man sits silently in an even bigger leather chair behind a massive old desk. The git, clearly scared of the old man, introduces the old fella to Dookie as 'Don Zukabug', and looks to Dookie to introduce himself to this big wig. Dookie, clearly looking to make an impression, reaches out his left arm and grabs the git by the scruff of the neck. He punches him in the face with a rounding right hook, drags the man to the window and throws him through the glass onto the street below.

Don Zukabug slams his hands on the desk and shouts out, "God damn it! I knew your face didn't fit!"

Dookie turns to him and calmly sits down.

"It's not about my face! It's about what we can do together!!"

Don Zukabug listens to Dookie as he explains what happened to him, his men, and his kidnapped boy. He then offers Don Zukabug the chance to increase his townsfolk numbers, meaning more building work, more taxes, more jobs and less inbreeding. He just needs some armed people to help create the illusion of a much larger force than just the fifty Warriors he has. And any info on the local GreenBacks. Don

Zukabug agrees to exchange info, at this point.

===

The local GreenBack info;

The main GreenBack is a total twat. She goes by the name 'Aska Aska' to her followers. He points out of the broken window to show Dookie the edge of town and the 'drop off', as he called it; a cliff that marks the edge of the sandy wasteland. At the bottom it's all lush green valleys and GreenBack controlled towns and villages. Would be great if not for their greedy green iron fist, he explains.

===

He tells of her troops always scaling the cliff at the edge of town and attacking the water supplies or fuel dumps.

"They try and make us go without so we will surrender to them and become another ruled over town. But we are free folk! Fuck em'!"

He calms down and shows Dookie pictures of an area, almost right below them, at the bottom of the 'drop off'. He points to a location and explains that she has a massive compound 'Las Ranchos' down there, with slave guards and a small jail for anyone that gets out of line with her.

"That's where your boy will be, I bet." he states.

Dookie shares his plan with Don.

THE PLAN OF ATTACK

While his armed town folk shoot up one side of the GreenBacks' compound, Dookie's men will concentrate quietly on the other side. As most of the guards will be forced to repel the townfolks' supposed attack, Don's people will enter the compound and bring the fight straight to her living quarters. A few of Dookie's Warriors will take care of the guards shooting back at the town folk, while the rest clear their way through the buildings and jail house. Once clear, the town folk can offer the survivors of Aska Aska's guards a safe haven in the free town above. They can then take what materials can be carried back up with them. Then, Dookie's guys will blow the place to hell.

Dookie ends the plan with; "If the boy is there, great, we'll take him with us. Whatever cash or gold is laying around we split fifty-fifty between your town and my crew. That'll be the end of our joint venture. If the boy isn't there we will continue on to the next compound on our own. Deal?"

The boss jumps to his feet, holds his right hand out and shouts, "Deal!"

The new teammates agree that both sides need time to prepare for war. Dookie's Warriors need a few days to rest and recuperate. The Don says they can all stay in his hotel and the townsfolk will all pitch in with helping to feed them. He also states his townsfolk will use this same time period to sober up.

As the two men bond over their new venture, Dookie apologizes for throwing the git out the window. Don Zukabug assures him the git was a treacherous GreenBack spy, who he had been feeding false information to for months. They both have a good laugh about it, and Don takes Dookie around town to introduce him to everyone and tell them of the new plan.

The townsfolk welcome the news, as they hate the GreenBack bastards as much as anyone. They also hope to get some of their family and friends back from the cruel Aska Aska and her army of Money Grabbers, known as M.G.'s

Over the next few days, the townsfolk sober up and Dookie's Warrior hoard rests their feet and backs and cleans their weapons. The townsfolk also insist they bathe each day, and they wash the warriors' clothes in efforts to rid the small town of the stench the men brought with them. Dookie and the guys are amazed at how friendly everyone is. Don Zukabug explains to them that whenever anyone moves on from the little town, two things are asked of them; to spread the word of how scary and lawless it is there. This keeps the marauders from thinking they are an easy target. The second is to never confirm their location. This helps other townships along the basin ridge too.

With all the prep work done, everyone sober and rested, Dookie and Don decide to strike early the next day.

LAS RANCHOS WAR

Early on Tuesday morning, just before the sun is up, the invading force of free people slowly lower dozens of long, long ropes down the cliff face. Dookie and his men quickly rappel down and set up a perimeter. The townsfolk follow on down the ropes. Once at the bottom, Baron and Joey help set them up amongst the brush, rocks, and trees on the northern side of the compound. Once the two hundred plus townsfolk are in position, locked and loaded, Baron and Joey make their way sneakily back to Dookie and the warriors.

A few minutes go by. The Warriors wait anxiously to hear the attack begin.

BANG!

A rocket grenade lands slap bang in the centre part of the main building, and as it does the townsfolk open fire in unison, lighting up their hiding places with the flame of freedom spurting out the ends of their rifles. Dookie watches on as the GreenBacks and M.G.s congregate like the paid-for monkeys they are, at the northern border of the compound. Dookie signals to his men. Move in.

Like ants swarming on a dropped ice cream, the Warriors take the headquarters, armoury, and jailhouse. They also took out the northern defences from behind to let the townsfolk in. Dookie homes in on the screams and commands of what could only be Aska Aska on the radio requesting help.

He shoots, kicks, punches and head butts his way through her defences followed by his three most loyal buddies. They enter the decadent throne room. Bedazzled with jewels and gold their enemy retreats through the side doors. Rusty points and shouts.

"Dooks over there, over there".

Dookie raises his gaze along the arm of his buddy and across the room to where he's pointing. Just under the throne hides a boy. Dookie calls out to him.

"Xris, it's dad! I came for you boy!"

The boy springs to his feet and runs to his old man's waiting arms. They both know there's no time to talk. Xris reaches his hand out and Dookie reaches into his large camo leg pocket and places his favourite little Uzie in his son's hand.

"I've saved that one for you dude! more magazines in my packs right pocket. Now let's tear this bitch a new arsehole!!"

The boy joins the four Warriors as they plough through the lavish home of the kidnapping Ask Aska. Dookie, now happy as a pig in shit pauses from his rampant killing spree of GreenBacks and M.G.s to consider his agreement with the townsfolk.

He sends Joey back to the cliff face, gathering the troops and freed hostages as he goes. He sends Rusty to oversee the removal of wealth from the bitch's home and Baron to gather some of the stragglers up to assist the wounded, friend and foe, as he retreats with orders to invite any M.G.s to a new life in the Freetown above.

The father and son, however, keep on ploughing through the bitch's defence for another ten minutes. It feels like a lifetime to her M.G.s; her troops begin to surrender to the almost relentless anger and power of the two scariest bloodthirsty freaks they have ever witnessed. But just as they grab the fat, ugly GreenBack bitch, Aska Aska, her reinforcements arrive!

Dookie stands tall over her as he forces the monstrous wench to her knees. His trusted ka-bar pressing against her carotid artery. His boy, by his side, reloads another banana clip into the Uzi and holds it out for the uninitiated reinforcements to witness, as they tread over the twitching corpses of their fallen comrades.

An old GreenBack dismounts her M.G. powered tuk-tuk and approaches. Xris whispers to his dad, "Fuck! It's her mother! She's got more power, more M.G.'s, and more coin than this dull bitch can dream of. We're fucked dude!"

Dookie doesn't flinch. He keeps his thousand-mile stare locked on his new foe. She stands confidently just five or six feet from them; her hoard of whimpering quim stays some ten or more feet further back. She begins to demand her daughter be returned with immediate effect. Dookie and the boy stand silent.

"You must know, you've lost. You're outnumbered, outgunned and surrounded," the wrinkly old GreenBack states.

Dookie calmly and loudly retorts, "A great General once said, when told he and his troops were in a similar position to us now, the good news is we can shoot in any direction and hit the enemy!"

The nervous M.G.s back away further, scared they won't make it home to their ill-gotten gains and stressed-out families. Then Dookie, realising he's got them on the ropes, looks around to intimidate them a little more. The old hag notices him taking his eyes off her and lunges at the boy and drags him to her side. The boy pulls the trigger and empties the clip as he's torn away from his father's side. A few rounds wound the old hag but not enough to put her down, the rest take out five more M.G.s

A stalemate. Neither side budges. You could hear a pin drop. Then the boy places his Uzi on the floor. He locks eyes with Dookie for a few seconds and Dookie knows it's over. He eases the pressure on the blade pressing against his captive's neck, takes a deep breath and begins to negotiate.

He tries to negotiate his son's freedom, but the GreenBack hag won't hear of it. In the end he pulls his Glock nine millimetres from its holster and pushes the barrel to Aska Aska's head. He steps just arm's length away from her and the old hag allows the same distance for the boy as she keeps her menacing grip on him. They speak quietly for just a few seconds.

The boy reaches out a hand to Aska Aska, and as she takes it, he pulls her toward him. Dookie removes the barrel from her head. She stands to her feet and matches her mother's line. The bitches stare Dookie down with ferociousness, but as the old hag turns to her commander, and begins to order Dookie's assassination, the commander's head explodes! Blood splatters everywhere.

The hag, now with a face full of brain matter and bogies, turns to Dookie. "What the fuck!" she screams at him.

Dookie replies, "That's the power of a fifty-calibre sniper rifle, bitch. If you thought I didn't have backup, you're wrong. Now here's the deal. The boy has agreed to stay, with terms…"

He rattles off a small list of demands such as no unwanted sexual advances from her pedo daughter. He is to be free to wander the compound alone, etc. No retaliation should be brought to the people of the town of Light or his company of Warriors, and finally, for Dookie to be free to retreat up the cliff.

The GreenBack bitches mull the demands over. They retort with an additional demand of their own, for Dookie's life to be death to be held off. He must leave the town of free people above within three days. On the fourth, they would hunt him down!

Dookie winks at the brave boy and agrees to the terms. He begins to step backwards and away from the enemy, forced to leave his boy back in the hands of the unhinged bitches. They too back away slowly into the ranks of the M.G.s

Dookie watches them disappear, down the dirty tracks for a short moment. His world has just imploded on him, again, and in that quiet moment it begins to hit home. The tears run down his face, and he gasps for breath. What does he do now? How does he live? How could he have let this happen? He just stands still. His mind goes into overdrive, beating himself up over and over again. This trauma will walk beside him for eternity. A deep breath. Another. Another.

The Warrior in him needs to come to the surface and take control. He slows his mind and his breathing down. He counts down slowly in his head. 10, 9, 8, 7, 6, 5, 4, 3, 2, 1, zee-mother-fucking-row. The Warrior brute regains his composure. He turns and walks back to the cliff face, grabs a rope and his crew of loyal Warriors pull him back up to the town of free people.

His crew console him for his loss as do the townsfolk. He goes back to his room and washes the stains and stink of blood and guts off his skin. That evening the townsfolk hold a vigil for the fallen souls lost in battle. They install a wooden monument on the main road with the list of all the men and women who have given their lives for the fight. They include Dookie's boy on the list, a nice touch he thinks.

Don Zukabug holds a toast to the Warriors and invites them to make a home and a new life there in the town. With the money, ammo, and guns they've stolen from Aska Aska's compound they can all live a little better and feel a little safer.

The men look to Dookie for guidance. Should they stay? Will he? He explains to his men and Don about the arrangement with the GreenBacks but believes it's a great place for them to set some roots down. He also suggests they could build lookouts on top of the cliff to watch for any future attacks and become the guardians of the township. Most of the men and Don agree.

Don Zukabug, Rusty, Joey, Baron and Dookie hatch out plans for plots at the edge of town for the new timber frame houses to be built for the Warriors, along with a few little shops, two lookout towers over the cliff face and a police station. All the townsfolk have pledged their support to help with the builds and orders have been sent out for the first bits of construction. The money 'liberated' from Aska Aska will more than pay for it all.

Friday morning comes and Dookie makes sure he has a good shower and massive breakfast as he doesn't know when he will get to have either again. His pack full of supplies and webbing full of loaded magazines for his M3 with five grenades to launch from it. Two boxes of fifty calibre rounds in his cammo's cargo pocket for the sniper rifle his Warriors insist he take with him, his trusted Glock nine with two mags and his beloved Ka-Bar.

He leaves town early with very little fuss. Sneaking out before most people are up and about to ensure he makes the mountains before the M.G.s get to him. He keeps a fast pace all day, barely stopping at all, and makes it to the first rocks south of the township by nightfall. He digs himself a little sleeping pit and pulls some bushes across it as he collapses down to sleep. His first real night alone. He is so tired from the twenty-hour hump across the flat baron lands he just basically passes out.

He wakes at first light and crawlsd out of his hidey hole. He takes up position on a high rock to look out at where he's come from the day before. He can see the M.G.s convoy. They aren't walking. Lazy fuckers have pickup trucks. And they aren't far off. Time to test that fifty cal. out he thinks. Standing proud on the rock he loads up the weapon with the three rounds it would hold. He takes aim at the centre front of the lead vehicle. Squeezes the trigger and throws that first round down range.

Direct hit! Smack bang into the centre of the radiator grill. The truck rolls to a quick stop and begins to smoke. The M.G.s disembark the vehicle like rats from a sinking ship and congregate at the tailgate end. The other truck slams to a stop too. Dookie cocks the bolt back and takes aim again. The second truck is rendered useless too, with the second-round whipping through its engine block. Now his enemy must hump through the remaining sand as he has.

Now he knows. Twelve men follow him. He grabs his gear and makes his way to higher ground. He makes camp around noon in the cool shade of the mountain. He spies through his binoculars again over the land below, to witness his followers just getting to the first rocks. Again, he loads up that fifty and aims for groups of the M.G.s standing one in front of each other, like the untrained morons they are. Dookie pops a round off and takes out two, centre chest with the first round. The others duck and run for cover. They wait. So does Dookie. He sits and watches them hiding, too fearful of his aim to move. Meanwhile Dookie snacks on a muffin and a bottle of juice.

Twenty minutes go by and the first M.G. boldly moves from his rocky hiding place. Dookie watches him waving his hands at his men, telling them to get up. Dookie puts a small entry hole in his back and a large exit wound in his chest. The enemy M.G. falls to the floor. His men aren't going anywhere for a while now. Pussies, Dookie thinks to himself. He gets his pack on and keeps on up the mountain track. As night falls that evening, he tears some leafy branches off some bushes and uses them to conceal his bulky mass as he sits out on a ridge. His enemy has barely moved at all. He watches them as they make a campfire and cook their MRE's.

The next day he makes and sets a few traps on the path. Nothing to 'killy', but a few little dug out holes covered with leaves will sprain an ankle or two and slow them down even more. He sets five traps and two work. Two more of his enemies aren't in pursuit anymore plus one more to assist them. Twelve have become six. Dookie leaves the pathway and heads for some close by gnarly looking rocks. He nestles in and spends the night. The next morning, he stays put. He waits for the six to pass his position.

He watches them all day. These idiots are just following the natural course of the mountain. They haven't even noticed Dookie hasn't been through yet. They make camp in a clearing near a little stream and set up a fire, cook their food and five go off to sleep. Leaving one on fire watch, on what should have been a two-hour stint before he wakes the next guy to take over. However, about an hour and a half into his shift, Dookie creeps up on him. He quickly wraps his right arm across the M. G's face, gripping his hand into the left side of his head by the man's brow and pushes his left hand to the base area of his skull. With one fast almighty push and twist he snaps the unlucky fella's neck.

He leaves the man, hunched over himself and balancing on the rock on which he'd sat for his fire watch. Dookie then etches a note in the dirt to the remaining five just in front of their murdered buddy.

'Go home'

He retreatsinto the forested canyon and spends the night watching on from a distance. The five wake from their lovely full night sleep at first light. Dookie can see them panic when they see the dead watchman. They run around like headless chickens with their weapons pointing at anything and nothing. The fear is ripe in them. And so, it should be. They know Dookie isn't going to give them a choice again. They pack their shit up and head back down the mountain like scared little bitches.

Dookie watches them head back down the mountain pass for the rest of the morning. While he does so, he sits up on some large conveniently placed rocks and takes a nice slow moving and well earned dump.

All our battered hero must do now is keep moving.

Battle weary & tired, he makes his way calmly and safely down the returning side of the mountain range and past the old southern frontline, the GreenBacks have enforced for years. Now, just open land and a small river where some people had used the old destroyed Head Quarters buildings and pieces of military equipment, left behind by the fleeing GreenBacks, to convert into the bases of new homesteads for their families.

Dookie stops and rests there for a few days, but knows he has to keep moving further south and east. East back home. He's walked for so long, days have turned to weeks and weeks into months, stopping in villages to rest, but never for more than a few days; just in case. Forever present is the thought of more GreenBacks trailing his scent.

The loneliness grows on him, he reminisces to himself about the buddies he once had, the battles and skirmishes, the friends he's made along the way. They would be great memories too, if not for the overwhelming sense of loss. That boy. That war. His men. His Corps. He's lost it all.

Some Days the grief takes over and he just sits all day, all night, staring into nothingness. Fighting his inner darkness each time, he struggles through those moments, believing there must be some reason for it all.

Better be a good reason. Over and over in his mind he relives the last time our crumbled hero saw his son, how the boy, young and scared, picked his broken father up and told him "It will be ok dad" and facing that insurmountable force of those 'GreenBack Bastards' the boy walked heroically back into the torture chamber of the ugly 'Aska Aska' ogre to guarantee the life of his father and his battling Warriors. Dookie lost his boy and the war... or was it just another battle?

His boy, now once again, lost to the perverse GreenBack and her mind twisting darkness. Our hero can only pray that his boy's mind stays open to the light.

Alone, Dookie fights through the darkness and the voices calling him in. He concentrates on the light. He's seen people, good people walk into the darkness. It changed them. He tries to set out a new plan in his mind's eye. If not for himself, for the boy.

"There must be some reason I'm still here in the light." He thinks. He believes.

Stranded in the southern desert wasteland he has no choice. He continues through the dirty sand for freedom, finally into the coastal lands and finds higher ground to secure. He calmly sits on a mountaintop. Breathes the fresh, crisp air and tries to empty his mind.

He waits with a watchful eye from his high perch, for a chance to come out of hiding. And, after weeks of waiting, he spies sails on the distant shore. With giddy excitement he all but rolls himself down the mountain at the highest possible speed and wades out into the ocean to greet the vessel.

Once aboard he offers to trade his security services as protection from pirates and offers to help out wherever he can in exchange for transport east. The captain accepts his offer and finally breaks Dookie free of the western lands and rides the tides back home.

Once back on the shores of his rainy homeland Dookie retreats further southeast, back to the Dragon Valley where a crumbling capitalist society has been pushed to the brink.

Part 2

THE SNOWFLAKE REBELLION

Now back home in Dragon Valley, as if just breathing wasn't hard enough for our hero, the realisation that his life is in ruins is almost too much. He has nothing but a floor which his family has lent him to sleep on for a while. He's on an airbed with two leeks, as if enough air doesn't come out of his ass during the night, eh?

"Better than a cardboard box though," he thinks to himself.

Still, he ploughs on with life. A new mission to save some cash so he can go hide the rest of his days in a remote rainforest. Seems like penance, but it's the only step forward he can take. The only place he sees light.

Then, whilst drowning his sorrows in a bottle of vodka she enters his life again. A meeting years ago had stayed with him. He liked her. He likes her. Let's cut to the chase, like all good heroes he gets the girl. They form a bond that gives him light and belief once again. Is that happiness he feels? Unlikely as it is, he breathes again. Like a stream becoming a river, life's blood fills him. Strength. A man reborn. A fat man, but still… a man.

Now wanting the quiet suburban life, they plan a stress-free existence. Both working shifts and building a new life in a normal town. Our hero lands a 'job for life' at a local Hellmart marketplace. They have been popping up everywhere over the past few years and so believe this is it. Mediocrity at its best. He'd stay there treating it as his retirement gig, stress free and happy.

Our hero, Dookie, works in the security department. Stopping shoplifters and any other punk that thinks they can push the staff around at Hellmart. He's found his calling. Tossing robbing idiots down the steps, choke slamming the odd abusive moron and even taking on a coke head with two rottweilers all in his first few shifts. What a great new way to vent the darkness inside. His time in the corps has put him in a good place to deal with twats, junkies and robbing mother fuckers alike.

For the first few years he didn't give too much time or concern to the overall attitude of staff at his Hellmart market. Work was work,

"No one's happy about it, that's why they have to pay us right" He always says. But even so, the anally retentive way in which day to day activity is monitored and 'requested' is just... Well, something isn't right and it's getting worse.

They may not be building pyramids at Hellmart but my word they like to make a mountain of stress and work about putting shit on a shelf! And the fact they must pay us to do it doesn't half fuck them off to no end. Clearly there is something wrong with this place. The moral low ground has become the new normal. There must be some kind of dark forces at work here.

A growing concern has became an investigation for our hero. Over time the market has came under new management at local and corporate levels and things have quickly gone from bad to worse. Local staff and customers are beginning to suffer at the hands of the new corporate boss, Di the Dastardly Dick.

=====

Di the Dastardly Dick;
Making his fortune over the past thirty years selling socks

and willy warmers to retailers worldwide, he sold his business off suddenly right before Hellmart announced him as CEO. Hellmart staff, shareholders and customers alike were hopeful with his appointment at the head of the company.

Tale of the tape:
5'11"
Carnivore
Married with three kids. Two aren't his, but shh! He doesn't know.
Penis name: graham
In brief.
Since selling his company he has distanced himself from friends and family who now don't even recognise the grim figure of a man who stands before them. He now makes so much money as head of Hellmart he has his favourite morning cup of tea blended and flown in each day one cup at a time from India.

===

Di the Dastardly Dick got right in to fucking the business up from day one. Working hours at the marketplaces across the land were slashed yet the number of days that staff were expected to work went from five to seven. Contracts of employment changed too; so called, 'flexible' contracts so the bosses can tell staff not to come in tomorrow or stay later today. Everything favouring the corporation, never the staff. Many of the long-standing older members of staff have been bullied out the door then replaced by computers or with younger staff who were accepting just seven hour per week flexi jobs out of desperation to buy food and some sort of shelter.

Prices of everything went up and therefore lifelong customers were forced to shop elsewhere. Soon computers replaced staff wherever possible, even serving customers in some cases!

Management faced changes too. Some of these happened right before our hero's eyes. Like Miguel, the floor manager. A day our hero will never forget!

Miguel, the floor manager, is a little fella with a big man's attitude. He comes in daily and publicly berates some underlings like the contract cleaner for instance, just to get his juices going and ensure the stick up his poop shoot is properly lodged in for the day. He walks around the market twitching his head as if he's about to explode. His arms curve out as if he's carrying invisible carpets as he paces the market. All the staff avoid him like a Covid cough. He seems very happy and content in himself. The elusive market leader is so proud of him. She holds a meeting each day so the other managers can applaud him.

One day there's a visit. A visit that will change everything for Dookie and Miguel. One of the Corporate higher ups has come to the marketplace. Dookie watches this boss type walk the marketplace with Miguel. They go from stall to stall inspecting cleanliness and product offers for some time.

Then the big boss stops at a tinned food stall and points at a stacked can of beans on a shelf. He starts crying and shaking in a fit of rage! He then begins going mental at Miguel about two specific cans of beans facing the wrong way. Storming off like a toddler in a rage to the back area. He explodes as he enters the warehouse. Growing to 8' tall with horns protruding from his head and claws for hands! Dookie can't believe it!

Dookie whispers out loud to himself "It's actually true! He's a demon! Evil runs this joint! It all makes sense now."

Then Dookie watches on as the demon boss reaches down and grasps the floor manager, plunging his grip deep into Miguel's anal cavity and with a scooping motion he picks him up, stretching his evil arm out to locking point over his horny head. Miguel slides down his arm only stopping just past the elbow! He screams out in pain and the demonic boss throws Miguel down to the ground.

"Ooo nobody deserves that."Dookie thinks.

Then the demon releases his internal grip and rips his arm from the stretched hole. He flicks his shit and blood covered hand over the walls and then steps back a few paces.

Miguel lays crying and twitching on the floor grasping at his precious bum bum. Then the movement of the sad little man becomes erratic, squirming and shuddering into a blur, the cameras can't keep up, he's transformed. Like a scene from a Disney movie. The now flaccid, tearful Miguel rises up and spins around at great speed and *BOOM*! A reincarnation! A new body! No broken bones! No bleeding anus! A miracle! A whole new guy stands before the demon. A scrawny, tall fella wearing ankle swinger trousers and a white shirt.

The new floor manager, Nikel, has arrived!! The demon returns to his human form. He concludes his visit, introducing Nikel to the staff and leaves the premises.

Our hero has no idea what to do. Who can he take this information to? Who can he trust? He keeps it safe and decides to keep building his evidence on it.

Let's take a look at Nikel.

====

Nikel;

A man's man. Generous as hell. All smiles. He can't do enough for you. These aren't the sort of things that are said of Nikel. More like, miserable as sin. Haemorrhoid of a man! Dick wad.

Tale of the tape:

6'

47 years of age

Breast fed until 7 years old

No discernible qualities

Blends his food when at home so he can suck it through a straw whilst swinging in his man-sized papoose

Was reported missing for 9 years but returned around eighteen months ago with no memories of his missing years.

Now married to a discounted mail order bride, Gertrude, who just moved her first husband and three children over from an unspecified country. Nikel sleeps in the garage as there isn't enough room in his house.

Enjoys competitive cross stitching

Penis name: shames

In brief:

Although he's always been a mummy's boy bell end, Nikel used to be a fun-loving scuba diver. Taking holidays to remote beach resorts around the world. Nothing was better to him than keeping it 'au naturel' on the beach and doing a bit of skinny dipping. But after his best friend, holiday companion and mother, died about ten years ago he clammed up into the reclusive anal prick he has become today. His father bought him the deformed ex-suicide bomber Gertrude as a last-ditch effort to save his child from loneliness but has since given up on his disgraceful son.

===

Over the next few months at Dookie's Hellmart, the analness has become insane. Half the staff are now forced to ram sticks up their asses to ensure they enforce Nikel's regime.

"It's the rules" can be heard day and night in the now half empty marketplace.

The rules must be enforced! Bureaucracy has become more important than driving customers to the stalls. The Corporation has installed a huge number of remotely monitored CCTV cameras to ensure the rules are followed and Nikel has his underlings enforce his rule to full effect. Public flogging and shaming of staff who break the rules has become all too normal. Some fight the system, but punishment is hard and fast.

Many staff become too weak to continue the fight back against this tyranny and have been discarded or 'disappeared' since the age of Nikel, making it hard for Dookie to form a trusting alliance for his investigations. It isn't their fault. Starved from low wages, zero-hour jobs and high food and shelter prices, it was only a matter of time before any resistance collapsed. The remaining staff, forced to live with family and friends as rents and mortgages are a pipe dream of tomorrow, have been beaten into submission and the fresh-faced newbies are all of questionable substance it seems, ready to recall the cry of Nikel at any point... "it's the rules"!!!!!!

Dookie tries to infiltrate the hierarchy of the market, but the amount of ass licking, bold face bullshiting and general fake niceness that's needed to be pointed at the market's elusive local leader is beyond his capacity. She'll only feed on lies and darkness and Dookie just couldn't do it for fear of falling from the light forever. But if he can't get promoted in this way like all the unhappy lower leaders have, how would he know how deep the evil goes?

Time passes and Dookie's investigation is stalled like a turd in a back passage. He knows nobody would believe him without proof, so what to do? Then one day it hits him! "I bet there's an app for that!" He goes online and downloads the 'find a demon' app on his phone and now he can tell who an evil piece of shit is and who is just a twat. Awesome!

He decides to test it out straight away and finds that the lower manager holding power over him isn't normal. She's not just an utter bitch! He knows for sure now that she's a demon.

Let's have a quick a look at her and her favourite buddy.

===

Kimy;

The sort of woman you think of as a lady when you first meet her. Then you get to know her and realise that she's a sadistic bitch who gained her elevated position by pushing her predecessor down a flight of stairs.

Tale of the tape:
5'5"
Blonde
Consumes one piece of toast each day.
Consumes 3 to 7 bottles of red each day.
Must be always seemingly wealthier than the person to her right.
Hobby: creams horses dropping into jars and sells them as perfume online.

===

A proper two-faced demon with aspirations above her stature. She hates Dookie. Any chance to bully him or twist his job to seem as if it is to be terminated, she does. He can see her physically revel in his annoyance. She also has an ogre on her side. The feared-by-all admin ogre, Hellaina, responsible for many fatalities among the local Hellmarts. Our hero will spend years plotting against them. Using just enough of his bullshiting prowess to annoy them in return. Treating these two demonic twats as sparring partners he builds up his immunity to evil day by day during their head on collisions.

===

Hellaina;
An utterly horrific twat. Was besties with Miguel as she enjoys the public floggings.

Tale of the tape:
Born. January 1, 1804
5'7"
Enjoys: Nothing
Only eats raw meat
Cried so much as a baby, her parents tossed her over the fence of their backyard where she froze in a winter storm. Found during the 1950s by builders who were clearing land for a new housing project. She was thawed out and placed in an orphanage. Although they tried to get her placed with a family the crying baby turned into a whining child and then a disgruntled and violent teenager. Still in residence when the orphanage was knocked down in the 1980s she was forced

upon her local community.

Employed by Hellmart in 1981 after her local Hellmart leader saw her maul and permanently disfigured one of his staff for giving out incorrect change.

===

Dookie uses the app to view footage he found online and on market training DVDs to discover that the whole corporate level of Hellmart seems like it's now under demon management. The app has also proved the head of Hellmart is in fact the Devil incarnate. He now knows this evil runs through Hellmart from top to bottom.

With so much distrust and fear ruling over the evil empire of Hellmart, entire market divisions are slaughtered by the now all-powerful devils incarnate Dastardly Di the Dick. His temper tantrums and power plays have gotten violently worse and worse. The problem Dastardly Di the Dick is having is that being such an evil, money grabbing, power hungry ballbag, he thinks the rest of humanity is too. But absent to his knowledge is the simple fact; most of Dragon Valley just want a fair deal and a simple life.

Dookie has managed to fly under the radar and just out of Dastardly Di' gaze. His boss and her ogre buddy fall at the first hurdle, caught up in one of Dastardly Di's feeding frenzies. Never to be seen or heard from again. Luck! Maybe?

It's hard to find a positive in all this brutality, but Dookie feels a door had been pushed open during all the evil culls. What would this door let in? With the slaughter of tens of thousands of regular staffers and the loss of millions of customers Hellmart is on the brink. What will the king of willy warmers do next? Dastardly Di the Dick has truly ripped the shit out of the markets across the land. Cleaning house almost indiscriminately. Like a scene from a bad 80s action movie, the blood and bodies are everywhere. How can this be? Surely the lords of Dragon Valley will step in to help.

However, fortunately for our devil incarnate the land is ruled by plundering morons who spend this same time period butchering other parts of the population, especially the low paid, lame, or infirm, so they can keep more power, fame and fortune to themselves. They don't blink at Dastardly Di's brutal attacks.

Dookie survives the devil's next few waves of attacks. Standing tall and fighting back, he sustains injuries, yet somehow he's safe for now. He tries to help those that were injured in the atrocities, but most are now too weak to fight again. Some have lost their minds to the battlefields and now force out the cry "it's the rules", as they are firmly put under the long, thick, pulsating thumb of corporate law.

Finally, after such a long time the devil rests his axe. Dastardly Di the Dick slides on a new warmer for his cold little willy and allows the weary ranks to be replenished. The new staffers will of course have to sign the god-awful flexi contracts in the blood of their own mothers or first born. And thanks to the politicians and corporations hoarding all the money in foreign bank accounts well out of society, there are plenty of desperate souls ready to risk it all at the new style Hellmart.

THE SNOWFLAKES

Dookie's local Hellmart takes on replacements as do most around the Dragon Valley. Not enough though! It seems Dastardly Di the Dick only replaces one hour of work time for every twenty lost, for he wants what the politicians have. All the money!! What a dick Di is. The trickledown effect that has kept supply and demand circulating cash into society since the time it was conceived has become a proper drip. Monetary starvation has its evil grip firmly on Dragon Valley thanks to Dastardly Di and his narcissistic politician buddies. They've lost sight of how supply and demand rule our capitalist freedoms and by hoarding 99% of the wealth to just a few people the masses must and will rebel.

Some of the newbies at Hellmart are a different breed. They'd have to be. What normal person could afford a seven hour per week job? So, what are these beasts? They don't seem to be the type to rebel. Not quite fully man or woman. They can't articulate a conversation or look you in the eye. And they all have a phone addiction. Is this how our corporate devil dares to take the rest of us down? Replace us with these minions? Dookie keeps watch over them for any tell-tale demonic behaviour.

Nothing shows on the demon app, except bright colours flowing around them. What does this mean?

After months of observation Dookie just can't get a grip on a few of these individuals that congregate together like turds in a bowl. Nothing new is showing on the demon app, just the same bright colours. Most seem pretty average, whatever that is now, but a few stand out as extra special. He comes to realise these 'specials' aren't a threat. They're snowflakes!! It's the only obvious outcome. He's heard of this breed but never seen them up close.

Dookie watches on like a visitor at a zoo.

Who are these beasts with no discernible qualities, addicted to their communication devices and all fully believing they are 'the one'? Morons. It's obvious to Dookie that he hasn't been missing much. But these absolute fuck knuckles maybe the help our hero has been looking for. Surely underneath all the average Joe, unconfident, porn and gambling addictions and raised by stranger's freakish exterior, some of them must have some qualities he can use. Maybe he can train them. Mould them into warriors of some sort.

Our hero gets closer to the small tight knit group of Snowflakes to see what he can learn.

These few seem to be able to converse with one another confidently at will. Even when approached in a soft non-threatening manner, palms open and at arm's length, even by customers they do seem capable of speaking to others too.

Over the next few weeks our hero sits near them at break times. Getting closer and closer to them with each passing day, to help them acclimatise to his presence slowly. He sits quietly by, as they scoff down vegan sausage rolls and vastly oversized vegan puffy, not-quite-crisp things and swill strange purple 'smoothies' and discuss going out at the weekend drinking.

Intrigued by the notion of these morons being let out unaccompanied in the evening to drinking establishments, he seizes an opportunity on a rainy Monday lunch time to move right up close to one of the little male ones. As Dookie nudges up closer, the little snowflake shakes nervously but carries on with his lunch; mixed nuts and a zero percent fat yogurt. He quickly finishes his chipmunk snack and places his face firmly in the comfort zone of his vastly overpriced phone, then starts perusing pictures from that past weekend's festivities. Dookie can just about see the pictures as he leans in over the little fella's shoulder. He's stunned by what he sees. The males all went out wearing tuxedos and the females in evening gowns?

"Strange behaviour for a market pub," our hero thinks.

To make it more surreal one of the males dressed up as superman for no reason whatsoever and the others allowed this attention seeking dick wad to continue on with them!

"In my time we'd have slapped shit out him and sent the crazy little fucker home," our hero thinks to himself.

Still, if they can function like this together then there is hope for sure.

Dookie carries on with his lunch time observations. Listening in over the coming weeks he learns lots more about their primitive behaviours.

+They like to drink lots
+Most identify as vegetarians, but all eat chicken
+Evan the proper vegans eat chicken when they are drunk
+Most are virgins
+All addicted to online gambling and Porn
+Photograph each meal for hashtag Reasons

Above all else, these crazy little snowflakes don't seem to get too emotional about the job. It's just a thing they do and that's that. They seem to have been raised in a manner such that they know fuck all about the human condition. Well, raised may be an overstatement. Dragged up by the cheapest babysitter is more apt. But it's ok because they just had to have ridiculously overpriced toys, games consoles and phones so....basically they truly couldn't give a shit whatsoever, as long as they get toys they want. And they all want the same toys.

Back on the shop floor, Dookie watches one of them through his 'demon app' being berated by Nikel and.... well... nothing. The evil bile spurting out of Nikel, glows in powerful dark blood red through the app's lens but it just flows right over the ignorant snowflake. No effect! The snowflake just lowers his head and carries on as before.

Normally when Nikel howls out his passive aggression onto an average worker the powerful colours of death and destruction pierce through their body seemingly taking their heart and soul bit by bit.

Maybe these snowflakes have some kind of 'twat' defence? Whatever it is, this is awesome! Maybe a weapon in the making! Maybe, maybe.

Let's find out more about this group of snowflakes.

Here's the rundown of their profiles compiled as part of our hero's investigation.

===

D.C. - local snowflake leader;
A man. Well, Half. But one hell of a half. If hell has butterflies. Ladies, Gents, Swingers, Chimps that can sign. All are welcome at Dave's buffet of life.

The tale of the tape:
5' 9"
Skinny as a little rake
Humour; sometimes, but creepy
Mix race: veganish / human
Loves bum fun
You'll need wellies
Dates; international

Bad boy vegan

Penis name: slug

May need psychological help

Weapon: snowflake ninja stars

Training: His mummy won't let him

In brief:

This fixer upper is a doozie. Made to one day be on the headline news, DC has lived life to his max. Others may say "minimum" or "o right", but DC isn't just DC by name. The cosmos predetermined his exclusive individuality to liken him to comic book heroes such as Mr Tickle, Mr Bump or Pepper Pig so he's no snowflake like the rest of his pathetic age group. Sure, if you like a man that has an online and gaming profile to die for then look no further. However, like Raj from the big bang theory he can't actually speak to you ladies yet, but you'll get the drift when he hands you a wetsuit and puts his vegan snack down.

Likes / dislikes;

Likes: Large afro Caribbean ladies over the pension age with mobility issues due to weight or uneven leg length.

Likes: Tribesmen. Hunter gatherer types from the planes of Africa or India; it's more about the loin cloth and dirty skin.

Likes to be stepped on in heels.

Role playing is a must for DC's next partner. He loves games such as "railway sweeper vs train", "jedi and the storm trooper" and his favourite "dancing on ice" (you get to be the judge).

Dislikes; throat punches.

Dislikes: Getting caught in your house.

Dislikes: Meaty foods and quality lunch products. Nothing turns him off more than a ham and cheese sarnie. This would really put him off his oversized bag of vegan air puff fake crisps.

Mentionable notes;

DC does not use public toilets unless meeting a date there. He therefore confidently wears male adult nappies so he can go anywhere any time.

DC masturbates with ferocity up to eight times per day.

DC must always be kept away from monkeys, apes, zebras, and other seductive beasts, so days out should not be at the zoo or rainforest cafe. DC is currently banned from all rainforest cafes and all Dragon Valley farms, zoo's, monkey worlds and twelve Matalan shops.

DC uses 'Replens MD' moisturiser all over his body

Current crushes;

The queen, Sergei the meerkat, David Seaman, Lorraine Kelly, Cast of planets of the apes,

His next-door neighbour's grandma, His next-door neighbour's grandpa,

Chairman Kim of North Korea

===

Gorey;

This noughties missile is one for the ages. 'A great guy', 'cool dude', 'stud', 'the man' are all things you'll never hear around this misfit of society.

Tale of the tape:

Actual height 4'2 but appears over 6' due to his faith dragging him skyward.

Prolapsed anus

Six nipples

Born in nepal to an eighty nine yr old virgin

Dates: yes please

46

Penis name: it's complicated

Weapon: anal rosemary beads

Training: he's an MMA punch bag

A brief history;

A once talented MMA child fighter, he was once proclaimed to be the second coming of Christ by the recently deceased pope. Gorey became best pals and fuck buddies within the inner circle at the Vatican, which helped start a new chapter of his employment. A young energetic and self-confident Gorey rode not just one but a whole habit of nuns one by one into the Pope's future retirement villa, this young man had it all to live for. Then the accident changed his life's course from leader of faith and bringing the world together, to working in the shadows of a well-known high street marketplace. of course, he is doing so undercover for the Vatican, his first and only true love.

The accident:

During an MMA training session outside of the Vatican City walls Gorey was struck by a moped during his warmup run. As he fell to the cobbled street, the moped landed on top of him, the rear tyre spinning at speed ripped through his hot pink skin-tight shorts pulling his scrotum from his body and ripped the penis he loved so much in two... lengthways! Doctors operated on him for ages, even missing golf that day, but Gorey was left permanently disfigured.

===

Bree;

This anomaly of the 21st century was certainly born into the wrong time in history. Don't get me wrong, she's still a total snowflake fuck up, just that she should've been doing it in the 60's cuz she a proper party piece.

Tale of the tape

5'4"

Dates: "oh I'm just having fun, giggle"

Vagina name: the 18th

Dildo name: 5 Wood

safe word; supercalifragilisticexpialidocious

Weapon: doubled headed extended spinning hair curlers

Training: kung fu, pole dance edition

Always carries at least four STD's

In brief:

This greedy bitch hasn't had a good night sleep since her first sex education class. Like a massive weight being lifted off her shoulders, she finally realised what that thing was for and hasn't rested since. Guys, girls, objects, that one sexy looking pony. It's been an awakening. Using her talents and passion Brooke lived life to the full. But the burning?

After the clinic doctors medicated her & told her to slow down, she did and began to pray nightly. Believing her prayers had been answered when she started a new retail job and met some nice quiet playthings. Brooke finally smiled and could pee without it burning. Little did she know the pope's b&e team installed cameras at her place for an undercover agent who had caught her scent.

Mentionable notes:

Bree never wears underwear, just in case.

Her nightly "private time" has become the number one show on Vatican's channel 5.

All the snowflake guys don't stand a chance in reality. She's having too much fun riding the iceberg of femininity

She'll never be able to say her safe word because of the ball gag.

===

Getlan;

This cracker mother fuka is off the chain.

Raised by the original O.G. The gangsters all sing about, this lily-white bad ass was capping 9's at age six and downing 40'S by his tenth birthday. Mind you, Snoop Dogg did host his tenth and after that bong... young Get didn't have a clue what was going on til' he finally got up in that sticky icky icky! Yep. Syrup sponge and custard bitches!!!!! Snoop still holds out hope he will be around to witness Getlan pop his cherry but times running now Get's hitting his thirties. Does D.C. hold the key?

Tale of tape.

5'

Depressed

Should've been a hipster but couldn't grow the beard

Hero: sponge bob

Not sure but thinks he likes bum fun

Penis name: what's the point

Weapon: chopsticks

Training: judo albino belt

After the death of O.G. Getlan invested his inherited fortune in what he thought was a new boy band 'ISIS'. Turns out he fucked that up. HMRC took the mansion, boats, plane, and lands. The Bro's n' Ho's all bailed. Cleared of any terror activities, Getlan now lives like a monk with a short fuse and kinky obsession for trolleys.

===

Tupps;

This Tupperware loving wolly was clearly dropped as a child. In fact. He holds a world record since the age of just eight months old for the most dropped child; one hundred and eighteen times.

Tale of the tape.
5'8"
Hobbies: Tupperware collecting
Independent eyes so can see in two different directions.
Weapon: mobile phone with pop socket attachment bungeed to him to use as a whip. Or just in case he drops it.
Training: come on. Really
Fetish: naked Tupperware dancing
Virgin
Now working at Hellmart on the bakery stall, Tupps gets sent into the ovens to check if it's hot enough to cook the bread each day. He's lost his eyebrows but loves his job.

===

Hillbilly;

A complex man. An angry man. The angriest man in the land. Named hillbilly by his parents not solely due to the far reaches of his home from civilisation but after both of them, His mother, Billy and his father, Hill or Hillary in full title.

Tale of the tape:
5'11
inbred

spoon twiddler by trade

penis name: what the fuck is that Muma

weapons: spits bile that melts skin

training: doorkwando

Hillbilly lives some sixteen miles into the rabid wilds of the valley and twelve thousand feet up a mountain. He has a pet goat 'Herbert' who escorts him up and down the mountain each day for work and pleasure. Hill and Billy never leave the shack they built in 1902 but are glad their boy has. As the shack only has one room it's hard to "get your fuck on" ol' billy says.

===

The Snowflake Car;

The vehicle they mostly travel in is owned and operated by DC. It's a gigantic piece of shit. It burns oil and diesel so badly that if any of them don't recycle the world will boil within 3 days.

The car specs;

VW

Four door

Five speed (three actually work)

Three paint shades

interior -- eeewwwww

disco ball

lots of fake switches and neon lights

oversized amp and speaker

===

The Snowflakes Retro Siblings; Hipsters;

Our hero's investigation has also taken him into the path of one or two other stand-out members of Hellmart. They hang out with the Snowflakes from time to time but aren't snowflakes. It took some time for him to work out that these slightly older weirdos were originally deemed as normal humans, but as they grew up it became apparent, they were another sub breed like the snowflakes. In fact, failed snowflakes, due to their self-awareness. They wandered aimlessly across the lands to find themselves.

Finally, wearing second-hand cords and unshaven (yet shaped and waxed) beards they found themselves gathered in a trendy cafe in dragon valley ordering £8 bowls of cereal and skinny, soya, decaf mocha latte'. They are of course Hipsters. The self-away version of the numpty snowflakes. The cafe owner has since sold up her establishment 'The Rip Off Bar' and now resides on a cruise ship on permanent holiday.

These world savers come in vegetarian, vegan, vegan up-cycler and total prick. Let's take a look at the only ones that stand out as they are all basically the same as each other. It can be difficult to separate the male and female, nonbinary, transexual, cross dresser, self-identifying as objects, etc of these Hipster types. so, our hero has classed them as hipsters if they are generally smug as fuck, a bit scruffy but drive nice posh cars or spent four grand on a push bike, trying to be more self-aware than its worth, and like to self-harm.

===

Sausage;

If this guy gets any more hipster... well. Wearing the all too familiar beard of terrorist and the silly shirt buttoned all the way up with a non-matching equally stupid bowtie, brown cords with Mork and Mindy style suspenders pulling those trousers up just too high, so we all get to see a patch of nasty hair sprouting over the top of non-matching socks and either burgundy DM's or those ridiculous plimsolls that, we all hated wearing in primary school P.E. This guy is about as individual as an OralB toothbrush.

Tale of the tape:
5'11"
Identifies as 'a baby of the planet'
Rides a bike (a second-hand steal at two and a half grand)
Drives the Mercedes his gave him for his birthday at the weekends
Vegan
Loves sausages and M&S chicken
Vegetarian
Powers: lies like a mother fucker
Training: watches Bruce Lee films
Collects STDs
This guy's a real man of the people and eco Warrior. Except Saturday nights when he likes to get shit faced on imported spirits, wines and beers. He's not into all that local microbrew shit, ever since he got a nasty stomach bug that required an entire tree worth of toilet paper to sort out.

Has a large tattoo of a sausage on his right shoulder from a drunken night out in Amsterdam when he claimed his mother's sausage dinners were the best thing in the world.

Not much else to say about this bell end really. When he grows up and what not he'll be a decent fella. For now, he works with Tupps on the bakery stall putting holes in the donuts.

===

Lollie;

Ooh a hipster vegan upcycling lesbian. Shoot me now! She has three topics of conversation. Veganism, lesbianism, upcycling old clothes.

Tale of the tape:
5'5"
Identifies as an 'earth child'
Skier. But it's ok; she offsets her carbon footprint by giving money to a charity as that also saves the ozone layer.
Vegan but eats Nando's chicken
Is Bree's iceberg friend
Can't find out any more information as she won't shut the fuck up about being a bloody vegan. But she hangs with the others so...

===

The Meet & Greet;

Now that our hero had identified his prime candidates it's time to speak to them. Show them the truths of our land and get them to agree to train with him and combat this evil empire, save Dragon valley and perhaps the world.

How can he get them to listen to him?

Should he set up a meeting or something?

How could he get them to show up?

He's spent days thinking of how he can get them to talk with him. The only thing they have in common, from what he can see, is 'dull naivety' and that they seem to communicate like cyborgs through their phones even when in the same room as each other on some 'group chat' thing.

Finally! It hits him. Out of the blue he realises. If he joins this group chat thing posing as a potential shag to one or any of them, they would be stupid enough to do anything.

Our hero sets up a profile on 'snowflake book' and goes after some of the gang. It isn't difficult to get them chatting this way. Flirting away with little messages he then sets up the meet, the only way he knows they will all show up; He instant messages them all as a horny bisexual snowflake wanting a gangbang of course.

He calls them all to a secret meeting in an abandoned farm building a few miles away from the market, but will they really show?

They all show!

D.C. has brought protein bars, Lucozade, a wetsuit and twelve digital cameras.

Once all inside the building, our hero introduces himself.

"Hi guys, my name is Dookie and I'm the one that really asked you to come here tonight."

The Snowflakes and Hipsters are agasp at this betrayal!

Gorey shouts in a temper.

"This is bullshit! I was expecting a show."

He then exposes his deformity to the room, sits on the floor, pushes his headphones into his ears and begins to cry as Ed Sheeran calms him down, song by boring song.

D.C. calmly releases the handles to the wheelbarrow he's loaded his supplies into and begins to nervously shake. Getlan, standing next to him, reaches out his right arm and slides it up over D.C.'s left shoulder. He then angles his body toward his quivering bestie and simultaneously slips his left arm around his tiny waist, just below the belt line whilst his right arm continues to slip sensitively around the back of his neck. He holds him tight for what seems an eternity to our hero, watching on.

The rest of them stand, stupefied. Looking around as if it's a joke. Too scared to leave on their own in the dark, they stay. Waiting for the cuddles and tantrums to be done with.

Some twenty five minutes later, the horrific cries, foot stomping, tears and awkward cuddles seem to dissipate.

Then, in a tearful and broken voice Gorey finally asks the question our hero has been waiting for.

"Why?"

Dookie replies.

"I had to get you all here to explain something and ask for your help."

Gorey doesn't seem impressed. He pauses for a moment and looks to his friends with his hands out, palms up and shaking his head in disbelief he explains, "Oh, my actual god! This is the worst day of my life."

The gang all nod in solidarity. But as our hero thinks he's losing the room D.C. steps away from Getlan' embrace and says.

"We should hear him out guys. It may be important"

With that, our hero jumps right in and begins to explain the demon infestation issues and shows them the demo app and CCTV footage of Miguel being slaughtered and reborn as Nikel.

He has them. They're on the hook. Intrigued and scared they sit cross legged on the dirty floor and listen to the whole story.

"This is nuts! How can *we* help?" asks Bree.

"Well... I want to form a unit of warriors to help me take these fuckers out! You see, I believe these are real people, possessed. They need our help to be freed," eplaines our hero.

The group spring to their feet and huddle up like an NFL

team.

D.C. masturbates.

After the huddle they have questions.

Lollie speaks for the group.

"First off. Do we get outfits? Like the avengers or Fantastic Four? How are we supposed to help?"

Our hero chuckles, his belly jiggling like jelly on a plate.

"So! You're in then yeah? You can pick outfits if you want to. I reckon you guys must have something to offer the world other than YouTube videos," our hero states.

Getlan raises his hand and excitedly proclaims that he could render anyone unconscious with a flick from one of his chopsticks he always carries. He then pulls the chopsticks from his back pocket and flicks his wrist up toward hillbilly's head. With what seemed like a glancing blow from the sticks hillbilly falls to the floor! Out for the count!

Our hero claps his hands and shouts.

"Wow! That's gonna be useful"

The gang congratulate him on his precision as they de-pant the unconscious Hillbilly and begin to take pictures of his tiny penis.

"We'll get t-shirts made up with his knob on to screw with him for this weekend guys," Bree explains in a joyful giggly voice.

The gang all fall about laughing and agree this is the best thing they've ever done.

Hillbilly awakes, drowsy and confused. He pulls his pants up and stands to his feet, asking if he's missed anything. The gang laugh and tell him to behave.

Our hero asks them to spend the next few days thinking about the stuff they're really good at or about any special things they can do that may be able to help.

The group agree to meet back at the old farm building in three days.

Dookie is excited. It's finally happening, after all these years of waiting and investigating, he finally feels he can begin to unleash positive moral values and a teamwork atmosphere in the marketplace.

Would it be noticed right away? Would he get 'disappeared'?

RAISED MORALE

Over the next few days Dookie sets about making public his dismay at some smaller issues in the marketplace

He sets his sight on a small but significant item he feels all the staff will support him in. Getting the water turned back on! Who are these evil fuckers, Saddam Hussain!

The ever-failing water supply to the market is an annoyance for everyone. The taps in the toilets rarely work or work properly and the toilet flush is something of a Christmas event in the staff areas. Management always proclaims it's a bigger issue with parts unavailable or frozen pipes because it's cold or expanding and leaking joints in the heat but through the years these various issues only ever affect staff amenities, never customer ones, deli or bakery supplies. Bottom line, Dookie ain't washing his hands in the river no more!

Our hero waits for Nikel's lunch break that day. He follows him to the staff area and waits for him to start on his lunch; the usual floppy, sad, little plastic ham sandwich he eats every day.

Our hero pounces! Smashing through the door into the busy lunchroom he grabs a cereal bowl and begins to fill it with hot water from the tea urn. One of the checkout operators asks him what he's doing, and he responds loudly in a frustrated tone.

"Washing my fucking hands!"

He splashes his hands messily into the small bowl spilling water everywhere.

"I'm sick of going to the river to do this shit, this ain't some village in poorest Africa! we're supposed to be in a first world country with running water god damn it!!!"

The crowd of staff in the lunchroom all nod and nervously agree with him.

Nikel stands to his feet. Throws his floppy sandwich on to the lid of his little yellow lunch box and storms out of the room. Gone for just two or three minutes he returns, calm. Sits back down and returns to the sandwich without a word.

Dookie finishes drying his hands and begins to leave the room. All the while waiting for the shrill voice of the bell end, eating his floppy sandwich to scream out - 'my office Mr Dookie'. But it doesn't happen. Tupps enters the lunchroom at that precise moment and proclaims the water is on!!!! Showing his hands, clean as they are to the whole room.

Nikel shrinks in his chair.

D.C. masturbates.

Cheers ring out through the room! Nikel swallows the last of his floppy sandwich and leaves the room abruptly. A change in the wind maybe.

After the big water win, everyone is on a major high. Except for the hipsters who've decided it would be better if we milk, whiling only; rats, badgers and other such useless vermin and wash ourselves in their milk. Better for the environment and our skin they proclaim!

Unfortunately, it's a strange, usually quiet hipster type that has been the most vocal over the next few days. Petitioning this stupidity to management as he does, this weird confused little fella is taken to see the elusive market leader. When he re-emerges from her darkened office, he's wearing a trainee manager's badge and tells everyone he's being sent to a new market to train!??

Our hero is pulled, quietly into the staff training room by a few of the sad little manager types that same afternoon. They question and poke at him about the statements he made in regards to the water works in the previous days.

With the giant interrogation spotlight pointed directly at

him, our hero takes them on. Playing stupid, nice but dim, as if he doesn't recall. They have their paperwork filled out, their tight little angle to justify publicly flogging and then sacking him, signed, in advance by both the elusive market leader and Dastardly Di the Dick. They would have got away with it too if they hadn't got the date wrong! Stupid fucks. Our hero settles for an informal chat regarding the swearing, and they release him back to the wilds of the shop floor.

The winds keep coming along. The checkout operators ask for the boards to be taken down so they can see out of the windows again like in the 80s. Nikel, in this strange, weakened state he seems to be in, has his unhappy managers oblige. The market hasn't seen daylight since 1987 when Miguel threw his dummy out of the pram over the cleaners only cleaning the windows once a month.

As the boards come down the light forces its way through the layers of dust and grime on the glass to fill the entire marketplace. The staff and three customers are knocked back at the sight! Bats in the rafters take flight searching out new hideouts to rest and, yes, D.C. masturbates!

The powers that be quickly find out about this possible motivational moment and move quickly and relentlessly to cut all extra working hours on any market stall! Those hours will now be spent scrubbing the marketplace with scrubbing brushes inside and out. Weeks this goes on for. Forcing everyone in the marketplace to scrub and paint. Well, everyone except the cleaners and maintenance guys. They're left in the staff room doing fuck all! What is this madness?

The weeks tick by. Years of dirt are removed from the building not being cleaned and maintained correctly due to cuts and personnel mismanagement.

Now clean, the staff are ordered to paint. Soon it's gleaming with new white paint everywhere. The marketplace staff all blistered and tired now have to stand an inspection by Dastardly Di the dick.

Dastardly Di the Dick enters the marketplace with an entourage of suited men following him on their knees. Permanently poised at his posterior in hope to taste at least a fart, they hiss their lengthy and skilled tongues at the staff they begrudge employing so much.

Dastardly Di the Dick, stands on the back of one of these small, suited men, to address both the marketplace he's in and the many Hellmarts watching online. During his speech he spits lies about this 'relaunch' being part of his grand scheme along with his empire's failing share price.

"A new and improved shopping experience for our valued customers," is the line he uses.

As the broadcast finishes Dastardly Di steps off the ass lickers back and walks directly to the market leader, who is still just peeping out from the safety of her office. Her protective layer of managers parts ways to allow their beloved leader access to her. He stops just inches from the slightly open doorway and asks her, "Who"?

The market leader raises her right arm and points out of the door at Nikel. Talk about being thrown under the bus!!

Dastardly Di the Dick wraps his left arm around the shoulders of the quivering quim Nikel and begins to pace him to the door. Nikel, urinating down his right trouser leg, leaves a moist trail of fear as he's led outside.

The staff look on through the newly cleaned and usable windows as Nikel is laid out on the car park's tarmac. Forced down and heckled at by the excited group of morally corrupt ass lickers, the moist man freezes in fear.

Dastardly Di the Dick approaches his entourage's double

decker bus and steps into the driver's seat. He turns the key and revs the diesel engine. Blowing planet-killing smoke from the exhaust pipe he slams the bus into first gear and floors it! Laughing out loud he drives the bus straight over Nikel. Tump tump! The noise made by the bus's front and back wheels alike. Flat as one of his floppy little sarnies, Nikel looks dead. Truly thrown under the bus by the elusive market leader.

Dastardly Di dismounts the bus and his ass lickers clamber over themselves to sniff the seat he's left behind. He reaches down and picks the broken Nikel up and calmly says one thing, "This will cost another five thousand jobs."

He laughs and walks calmly to his private helicopter. Ushered in by his pilot they then take off and fly back to the dragons' capital.

The ass lickers take off in the bus; driving like maniac boy racers in the car park and hanging out of the windows flipping the staff off and screeching the bus's tyres as they hit the road.

Nikel, broken and crying like a baby, is left where he stood. Dookie seizes the possible moment of weakness in the broken demon and approaches.

"You ok dude? Do you need a ride home or anything?" he asks.

"No. Thanks though. That guys a proper prick! He'll get his one day," replies Nikel.

The opening is there! The man beneath the corporate demon is still alive and kicking in there. Maybe this is a step too far from Dastardly Di the Dick, because it certainly seems as if the man spoke then, not the demon! Maybe the scales have tipped.

It will be some weeks before Nikel returns to the market.

GAME PLAN! WHAT GAME PLAN?

Our hero and the gang of misfits step up training to every few days. Well, 'train' is a loose term to use for our bunch of misfits. Even our hero has no idea how to defeat the enemy. This, a major flaw in his plan, has become clear.

What a twat!

The snowflakes know. The hipsters know. The 'they couldn't give a fucks' know. Shit! Even the left wing 'let's all just get along' mums lot know!!!

What to do? Now our hero is in danger of becoming a party organiser for the snowflakes damn it. How is he going to direct this fight? He needs to find a weakness that doesn't involve running everyone over with a bus!!

He thinks back to the day he watched Nikel berate little D.C. and how it had no effect on him. How? Why? And when Nikel got 'bused' by Dastardly Di the Dick; he seemed to become sort of nice for a bit. What were these anomalies, and could they be turned into some kind of attack?

At the next meeting he tries to focus on this with D.C.

Whilst the other snowflakes discuss important issues such as how much better Call of Duty is compared to Red Dead Redemption, our hero side-lines D.C. and asks him about that day.

Dookie hands him his phone and D.C. watches the footage from the demon app and laughs.

"Oh yeah, I remember that day. Nothing could bring me down I was so happy," he explains. "I hadn't been in long when Nikel had a go at me. I wasn't really listening to him cuz I had just finished watching Scooby Doo at home when I looked out of my window and saw my neighbour at his... err I mean *her* window with no clothes on!!! First fully nude real-life chick I've ever seen. Milf dude."

Our hero turns to face the wall. Headbutts the wall three times and confirms.

"Wow. Ok. So, you were just really happy."

Now that happiness is confirmed as the reason the demon had no effect on the confused little perverse moron, our hero can make a game plan. Finally, for real.

He gathers the snowflakes together in an NFL type huddle and explains the new mission. He asks them all to be overly nice to everyone. No matter what. All the market staff! He iterates to them, not just the corporate demon dildos in line with Dastardly Di the Dick; they need to be nice and talkative to the rest of the staff too.

Sausage pipes up, "What, even the checkout staff??"

Dookie responds, "Yes, guys even that lot"

He goes on to explain he will be recording as much as he can with the demon app to see if anything changes day to day etc.

HAPPY SATURDAY

It's Saturday morning 08:00. The marketplace is quiet. Nikel unlocks the front doors and pushes them open. Dookie stands in the open doorway with him.

"Remember when we used to have a line of customers waiting to get in here boss?" he asks.

Nikel pauses for a second and answers, "Those were the days, eh?"

He turns and quietly walks away with his recently acquired limp to the back area. His head is hung low as he knows it's a dig at him and the regime he backs. The truth hurts, almost as much as the bus did!

One by one the snowflakes arrive throughout the day, each of them bounding in with big smiles and full of beans. Our hero follows them all throughout the day using the demon app over the CCTV cameras.

Giggling and skipping around like a couple of little girls he watches Gorey and Hillbilly doing no actual work whatsoever, but making a positive impact on those around them they definitely are. You can't help but laugh at the morons. Jumping between the market stalls tossing a bouncy ball at one another. Not like they have to worry about tripping up a customer as there are none.

The two Snowflakes skip around, encouraging others they encounter to join in as they bounce the little rubber ball towards them and throwing their arms in the air, ready to catch the return volley. The market stall staff parry the ball back to them and laugh together as the wollies wollupt into each other trying to catch it on the returning bounce as they skip past the fizzy pop stall.

Bree and D.C. are running amuck too. Messing around on

the bakery stall throwing flour over Tups. Dookie laughs ridiculously as he watches Sausage try to put the holes in the day's batch of donuts, whilst being caught up laughing along with the others.

Getlan stands at the front of the market, grabs the tannoy microphone and starts rapping like snoop had tried to teach him as a child. However... Middle class Dragon Valley issues don't have the same deep emotional angst as the lyrics spat by those from the poor tormented states of violence where snoop and the O.G. were dragged up. Therefore, it's funny as hell! From the misery squad on the tills to the demonic management, all are laughing.

Dookie captures it all on the demon app. The colours beaming off the possessed are amazing. Not so much dark mauve and black as usual, but some have orange, pink, sky blue, letter box red. This is amazing stuff. A real breakthrough!! To top it all off, although our hero hasn't witnessed it for himself, rumours emerge this afternoon that Nikel has been seen smiling and even the elusive market leader pops her head out of the office for two or maybe three seconds.

Short lived as it is, customers do eventually start to build up in the marketplace and everyone gets on with their jobs. Serving those precious, neglected customers as best they can, after all, the poor bastards are paying an extortionate price on the products.

Maybe teaching the snowflakes how to drop and roll or sweep a leg is all well and good but when the demons can just flick you across the room, it seems almost pointless. No. This newfound information may actually be useful. Happiness. Niceness. Friendliness. Seems like these may be the key to unlocking this mystery.

"Almost like having good morals is essential to a good life!' Dookie thinks to himself.

Towards the end of the day Dookie decides that they need to catch one! Experiment on it!

At the end of the week the team meets up again. Dookie congratulates the Snowflakes & Hipsters on a great job, and shares the news from the demon app.

The team makes a plan to get one of the younger manager demons to go out with them. They identify Nash, the lesser manager in charge of bread and baked good stalls as a prime candidate. Young, newish, most likely to be strong enough to fight his inner demon. So, they target him for the set up.

The young Snowflakes set upon him for a few days. Targeting him with niceness and all that silly shit. They load him up with as much happiness as they can thrust upon anyone in four days! Then they bug him to go party with them. They promise drinks, women, drugs... All a good little demon would want on a Friday night!

The young demon agrees to the Friday night out and D.C. agrees to pick him up first; then they'll supposedly go pick the others up.

The scene is set when the group arrives early that Friday evening. The abandoned farm building is rigged with a projector, a one-hundred-inch screen and surround sound courtesy of Gorey.

"Wow, where'd you get all this from dude?" Asks Dookie.

Gorey replies, "If I told you, you wouldn't believe me."

The gang, hearing this, look at one another, more confused than normal then look to Dookie for reassurance.

"By the grace of..." Our hero proclaims as he winks at Gorey. Then laughs and shouts out, "well let's rig up the restraints just in case, guys."

They all fall in line and get to work.

Our hero pulls D.C. to the side to set him on his way. With a reassuring pat on the back, he tells the young Snowflake it's all gonna be fine and to make his way back safe and sound. D.C. hurries over to his piece of shit car, jumps in, turns the engine over and starts bumping Katie Perry' Firework song! Our hero laughs as he watches little D.C. go off into the village. He makes his way through the narrow village roads in his piece of shit car. The disco ball and neon lights dance in the darkness as he goes to pick up the lesser manager demon, Nash.

Outside Nash's house he honks the horn twice. A few seconds later, Nash appears from the front door and walks down the garden path and toward the awaiting snowflake. From the doorway an older lady appears, waving her hand gently and shouts toward Nash, "Enjoy yourself son, try and relax yeah."

Nash jumps in the front passenger seat and looks at D.C., D.C., cool and calm, looks back at him and blasts the stereo. Thumping out of the massively oversized speakers was now Pharrell's 'happy'!!

After a few minutes of listening to this loud happy style of music, one stupid song after another and watching D.C. bop his head and tap his hands along with the music, the usually miserable Nash starts to join in. Bopping his head, just slightly, along with the Snowflake.

They arrive back at the barn after just fifteen minutes or so. D.C. jumps out of the car telling Nash to do the same.

Nash looks confused but the happy music is now playing around the barn and the large screen is playing the video to accompany the tunes! He lets himself out of the car and joins the snowflakes dancing around like a bunch of Ewoks.

Our hero looks on, from the darkness, ready to pounce if the demon kicks off. He can't help but be proud of them all. Holding their nerves as they are. Especially little D.C., there's more to this guy than the wolly he shows off to the world.

After a few cocktails, courtesy of Hillbilly. Loaded with sugary stupidity and lots of Vodka to keep the smiles going. The experiment is paying off.

Nash is loaded on happy music, happy videos, and happy juice. Plus, it seems he's actually enjoying himself, then just a few minutes later he collapses flat on his back!

Our hero and his crew watch on, worried, excited, scared! Getlan can't take the pressure and knocks himself out with a chopstick to the jaw and D.C. masturbates slowly for what seems an eternity to them all.

Nash suddenly collapses. Laid out on the dirty floor everyone pauses. Then his body flips over, his ass in the air and face on the dirty cobbled floor. A massive, loud, smelly grunt of a fart comes thundering out of the balloon knot and no sooner has the sound stopped than the whole gang witnesses the demon crawl from the back passage of his possessed host.

The mongrel shit covered demon in its natural form is an ugly, short mother fucker to say the least. With a twisted spine, skin covered in warts and giant claw like hands and feet. It stands at the foot of its freed host drooling and snarling savagely at the snowflakes.

It eyes them up one by one, looking for the tastiest looking rectum to rip into.

The snowflakes stand, frozen in shock from what they are witnessing. Then our hero jumps from the darkness and grabs the freakish demon fuck by its scaly wart covered neck. He picks up the three-foot demon to face it.

The demon quivers as he comes face to face with Dookie.

Scared, it cowers and recoils its claws scratching

"Oh no, no... Devil dog, oh no it's you".

Dookie raises his other arm and using a torch with the power of a million candles, which an old man, O Rhodiwan, had given him some years prior, he shines the brightness into the demon's eyes!!

The demon screeches out and flakes away into dust. The wind carries it off into the fields and Nash is free of the demon's grip. Slapping his hands together to rid them of the dusty residue, Dookie can't help but wonder what the dead demon meant by his dying statement.

Meanwhile, Nash, grabbing at his turtle's hiding place in pain screams out, "What the fuck is happing?"

He explains, in a confused and panicked manner, to the group as he grapples with the seeping tear in his behind, that he can sort of remember everything and that he just felt angry all the time as though he had no control over what he was doing or saying. He begins to apologize to all the snowflakes for treating them like crap.

The Snowflakes treat him like one of their own. They kneel beside the freaked out and shaking Nash, each place a hand on him and let him know it'll be ok. Bree starts to unzip but the others stop the nymphomaniac and advise her it's not the appropriate time to try and get laid.

Dookie, feeling finally vindicated in his years-long pursuit of righteousness, scans his eyes across the room with what must have been the biggest smile ever beaming from ear to ear. Not just because he has been proven right, but because he can now finally tool up and rid the dragon valley of all these colonic cretins!

As he continues his blissful moment of tranquillity, he notices Gorey texting like a madman and then watches the little snowflake fuck-up slink off to the back of the barn. What is he doing? Is he betraying the group in their moment of wonder?

Surely, he just needs a good old fashion clip round the ear and a whack of confidence on the back. Our hero follows him out back. As he gets to the muddy driveway Gorey is already full steam up the drive!

Dookie shouts back to Hillbilly, "Oi! Gorey just grand theft goat'd you bro!"

Hillbilly screams out in pain as he's never been more than fifty feet away from his beloved Herbert.

Our hero takes off on foot, his belly once again jiggling like jelly on a plate. Panting like an overheated lion, the fat bastard is going for it. You'd like to think he was running but... let's say it was a very fastish walk! He chases after Gorey even as he loses sight of him in the darkness, the stench of Herbert's neglect, now a trail to guide him through the dark thick brush of the valley.

An hour goes by, and our hero finally sees lights over the brow of a distant hill. As he reaches the peak he collapses in a heap. Steam bellows from his still wobbling and numb, sweaty body. He prays for water! Water that has been heated up of course with a little shot of coffee with some sugar and milk of course!! Donut wouldn't go a miss either.

It's been years since he ran anywhere. Up that mountain from the green backs to be honest. Why run when it's so much nicer to drive eh? Lazy sod. He wonders for a moment if this apparent demonic swathe taking over the local lands has anything to do with those GreenBacks?

He shakes his head. More. Again. He shakes his head and punches the dirt, as he fights back those dark thoughts of his past. He files the anger back in his mind. "Breathe," he says aloud. A few deep breaths and he calms himself down.

He collects his thoughts and refocuses on his traitorous snowflake.

The lights are coming from a private airfield. Gorey has broken through the barrier and is making his way to a private jet? Dookie follows him and moves in for a closer look.

The door to the jet opens up and smoke bellows out knocking Gorey back on the steps a little.

Like a baby elephant, Dookie tries to conceal himself in the small shrubs and short grass as he continues his frantic approach. Now attempting to belly crawl, his fingertips barely reaching the dirt to pull his sizable body along, his progress slows. A new tactic. Walrus attack! He folds his arms back and flops himself along at speed. Now right under the wing next to the stairs he can see everything.

The new pope, Frank, stands at the doorway and greets Gorey with a huge hug and kisses on the cheeks. Gorey kneels at his new Pontiff's feet and kisses his ring. The pope helps him up and they both move inside the plane.

Our hero pauses for a minute to let this new development sink in. I mean, the Pope? Here? Dookie gets his phone out and points it at Frank as he moves past the windows of his private jet. He switches the demon app on and watches for its colours to show. Frank is definitely a Demon ruled shell. The darkness coming off him is pure black!

As our hero moves in, it hits him; maybe this is where the tech in the barn came from! Gorey's not be betraying us, he's hooking us up! With that thought, our hero skips up the steps and pokes his head into the plane. Hopeful of saving the snowflake from a cavity demon taking up residency in his lower intestines.

What he sees he can never unsee. Plus, he's still got the

demon app on record so if nobody believes him, they can watch it. Cardinals, nuns, the pilot, all spouting off dark colours of the devil. Everyone on the plane seems to be infected, everyone except an older gent in a large wax over coat. Just at a glance anyone would know, this is the famous Vin Hoisin, Vatican assassin.

Frank and Vin Hoisin are spit roasting Gorey with the help of two cardinals who are physically spinning the snowflake around.

The debauchery goes on for around twenty minutes until the old guy has to take a nap. While he does, our hero calmly walks into the cabin, stepping ankle deep into gold goblets, plates, crosses, and jewellery laced with diamonds and gems then over the scantily clad nuns and priests to reach Gorey.

Gorey is laid back in a sumptuous soft leather reclined chair with a half-naked nun cuddled into him. Dookie lightly taps his dirty big boot on the snowflake's naked foot.

"Oh, you scared the life out of me then dude. How are you here?" asks Gorey.

Our hero tells of his heroic journey over the rolling hills and farmlands in pursuit of him using the goat's stinking ass as a beacon to follow. Still dripping with sweat, our hero downs a large class of holy water and asks Gorey to explain himself.

Gorey reluctantly starts at the beginning. Our hero listens on as he finds out about his friend's accident, love affairs with three cardinals, fourteen nuns and Mr Churchy-church himself; : Pope Frank in his younger years. He also learns that Gorey's full name is Igor Twatavinski and that he is a descendant of Dr. Frankenstein's helper 'Igor'.

He learns Gorey isn't even a snowflake, he's fifty three years old but looks so young due to his daily washing ritual in a mix of holy water and a very tiny amount of an unknown substance passed down the generations of his family tree from 'Igor'.

The final fact Gorey tells our hero is that he is actually an agent for the Vatican, working under Vin Hoisin, on the trail of these monsters. However, whilst starting to explain the details, the pontiff wakes from his nap and switches his tablet on. Then starts watching his favourite show on 'Vatican TV channel 5'. The Pope's entire delegation of perverts crowd round the dirty old demon bastard, and they watch together.

Our hero looks at Gorey with a stern stair and points to the door of the luxury gold plated jet. Gorey stands up, gets dressed and tells his real work colleagues he has to go. Vin Hoisin throws him an old-fashioned wooden torch and shouts out as the two make their way down the crystal encrusted, gold plated steps of the jet, to only light that torch when the leader is surrounded by its disciples.

As Gorey and Dookie mount Herbert the goat, Dookie states that it may be better to just tell the other snowflakes you flipped out and ran away like pussy. Gorey agrees and they make their way back to the decrepit barn.

During the journey back, Gorey tries to explain the perversity on the plane. He claims he has never seen anything like it before. In the past it has always been hushed up in back rooms, one on one like. Never like that!

Dookie can't help but laugh as he shows Gorey the demon app footage.

"They're all possessed dude!! But don't worry we'll help them next, ok?" Dookie tells Gorey.

Gorey thanks him, and the pair ride along on Herbert in silence. Trying to process the strange evening outcome.

Daylight os just starting to break through the night sky as they arrive back. Hillbilly runs to his goat with tears in his eyes. They roll around in the mud hugging and licking each other as if they have been apart for years. Gorey and Dookie stand in front of the gang of Snowflakes who are clearly waiting for answers.

Dookie explains Gorey has just flipped because he's a little bitch that got scared. The snowflakes join Hillbilly and Herbert rolling in the mud with laughter. Pointing at their buddy as they do so. Our hero wraps his arm around the big wally's neck and quietly tells him to suck it up.

Dookie then goes over and sits with Nash, nursing his sore anus, and explains the group's activity to him. He makes sure Nash understands that this is top secret shit and he is now part of the crew.

Nash takes it all in and agrees to help. In fact, he gives the perfect information: "Tomorrow night, well tonight then or whatever! The market leader is hosting a party for all us managers at the marketplace at 7:00pm. We all have to attend!"

Our hero jumps to his feet!!

"SNOWFLAKES!" He cries out. "It's on like Donkey Kong guys! Go home and get some rest, tonight we take back our market, our rights, our happiness!! Be here 6:00pm sharp"

The gang applaud this, and all go their separate ways to get some rest.

D.C. masturbates.

HOW BAD CAN IT BE?

Back home our hero wakes from his daytime nap and sits in his beloved, big brown leather chair next to his wife, Shaz. She raises her head from a crossword she's been working on to look at him.

"So, what stupid shit have you idiots been doing then? You stink of goat shit and I've had to wash the clothes you had on twice!!" she says.

Our hero calmly explains his evening's activities to her as he finally downs that cup of coffee he'd been dying for, hours before.

She replies sarcastically, "There's something wrong with you isn't there? Demons? The Pope? You just wandered into his plane?!?"

After more back and forth between the couple our hero gets his phone out and shows her the demon app footage from around the marketplace, the private jet and the horrific scene of an actual demonic beast crawling out of poor Nash's bum hole.

She finally believes him. Not just believes but thinks she's seen a picture of a demon type character that looked just like the one that crawled from Nash's brown star.

Our hero's good wife goes on to search through her myriad of shit novels, old magazines and cookery books to find one particular article about a businessman that went nuts after embezzling loads of money from clients and then went on a killing spree before getting run over, but the money was never found.

Shaz claimed the magazine was a freebee off a friend or her mother or something and she hadn't bothered to really read it but remembers the cover story stood out.

She pulls the magazine from the pile and stares at its cover. Then turns it so her husband can see it too.

An artistic impression of a demon beast is positioned on the shoulder of a man standing with a fist full of cash in one hand and an axe in the other. They both agree that it looks almost identical to the demon that crawled from Nash's poor little bum bum.

They sit and read the article aloud, taking turns as they sip tea and coffee from their steaming mugs. Maybe it was a true story? Certainly, seems to have similarities to their current situation. Money, power, greed, narcissism.

They track down the author on Snowflake Book and ask her if this is real and, if so, can they meet to discuss. The author refuses to meet but discloses that the book was about a friend of hers. She explains that he was run down by a robin reliant attempting to navigate a small roundabout. The three-wheeler crushed him, but as he lay there dying in front of her, she witnessed this creature crawl out of his back passage and make off down a dark alley.

She goes on to tell how, as he lay there grasping at his poop tunnel and gasping his last breaths, he said, all it wanted was money and power and he kept telling her to let everyone know he was sorry.

She had tried to explain this 'possession' to the police and even the church, but she was sectioned for six weeks and hasn't ever come to terms with what she saw or subsequently happened to her.

"Nobody cared! Nobody believed me! Even when I met Cardinal Frank he just laughed at me!" she exclaims.

"Frank, the new pope? He knew of this?" they ask.

She replies in length about the new pope frank being in town. Still just a Cardinal when it all happened, he came to see her but didn't seem to really care.

"He still charged me the £89 consultation fee though! In cash! Greedy bastard" she rants.

Our hero and his wife look at one another across the computer screen.

"Frank! It's him. It's got to be him at the top! It makes sense doesn't it?" our hero proclaims.

They thank the author and retire to the living room to discuss. They surmise that the new Pope Frank must be at the top of the evilness ladder. Maybe he knocked off the old one to get the top job.

They do a little research online. They find out that since taking power over the church, he's been meeting with heads of state and business leaders alike during an epic three-year world tour.

The couple flick through the biggest business leaders in Dragon Valley and the surrounding lands of Crusty Gorge and the Gasland empire.

They are shocked to see that most of the big business leaders and politicians are being controlled like Dastardly Di the Dick!

Our hero takes stock of this massive issue. It makes sense to him now. The richest people in Dragon Valley keep getting richer, as the poor keep getting poorer. The rights of workers keep getting diminished as well as their working hours. The once proud support system for the older and unwell is being dismantled day by day. Not to mention the whole land is being consumed by dark thoughts, road rage and a general ill feeling to one another. Crime rises every year yet less and less police patrol our lands.

Our hero sits back in his favourite chair for a while and thinks on how he is going to defeat everyone.

His wife hands him a bacon sarnie and a nice mug of coffee

and says, "I know what you're thinking... One at a time, babe. One at a time. Now eat that and shower cuz you really do stink!"

PARTY OF LIGHT

That evening he meets up with his new band of brothers and sisters. Hipsters, snowflakes and one miserable old sod brought together to bring happiness, peace and prosperity to the world! Well, their little corner of Dragon Valley at least.

He's chosen not to inform the group that he's become fond over the past months, that this is, seemingly, just the start of the fight back. It's now clear to him that this has become financial terrorism aimed at the workers of our lands by the demon-controlled bosses of massive corporations, churches, and politicians alike. Well, I mean... It wouldn't be the most motivational thing to tell them, would it?

The snowflakes and Hipsters all come dressed in matching uniforms with their names printed on the back. Black skinny fit stretchy 'jeans and the t-shirt they've printed up of hillbilly with his ol' boy out.

"Ha-ha Really." laughs Dookie.

The group surrounds him, and all hold their torches just like the one he's used the previous night.

Hillbilly explains, "My parents know all the odd bods round these parts, so I asked 'em about that O'Rhodiwan fella you got your powerful light from. My parents told me to stay clear of him. So, we went right round to his gaff!"

Then bree goes on; "So, we asked O'Rhrodiwon where he got that torch from that he gave you. He claimed to have never met you! Then told us to fuckoff after a twenty-minute rant. So, on our way out we saw these on his shelf. Figured he was a lying sack of shit, so we nicked em'."

Our hero chuckles!

"Yeah, he's a complicated geezer. Good job though guys. But

remember those are superpower beam lights. I mean, a million candles. No shining in your eyes ok."

They all laugh at him and his parental type of guidance and then begin to go over the game plan for the happiness attack;

Once the group enters the back part of the marketplace where the demon beasts will be partying, Gorey will set the speakers up. D.C. will manage the playlist. Sausage will infiltrate the a.c. unit and hold the projector, pointing it at the flattest wall possible, so the images will play out as big as can be. The rest of the crew will enter, torches on full million candle brightness then roll glitter balls out to every angle they can. Throwing them as if they were grenades.

Our hero calls out, "We'll spread the light as best we can and keep on smiling until the end."

As he does, Nash walks gingerly into the barn. His rusty sheriff's badge is still causing him pain, but it seems D.C. has paid him a visit and as token of good will and friendship, given him some of his adult diapers, so that's helped fix his anal leakage problems for now. But he does have a certain stench to him. Poor sod.

Nash hasn't just come to share how the new diapers have given him his freedom and confidence back though, he's here to help! He volunteers to prop a door open so the team can gain easy access to the party as he must attend. He's also brought a torch with him! It has a strobe light on it which he believes the demon freaks will hate.

He does ask the group to ensure they attack quickly as the tear in his brown star is throbbing quite substantially. He wants to go home and soak it, as quickly as he can, really.

The group welcomes him with open arms even though he pongs of poo.

The gang mounts up! Tupps loads his passion wagon with

bree, Lollie and sausage. Hillbilly and Herbert gallop off at full speed, while the rest of the snowflakes jump into D.C.s or Dookie's cars. The gang are on the road.

It seems like a long, quiet, tense drive down to the village car park next to Hellmart for all of them. They decide to pop into the local pub, 'That Place', for a bit of Dutch courage. After necking three shots of brand and quality unknown Vodka they each have a pee and the nervous little D.C. masturbates like a hyped-up speed freak.

Getlan, bathing in his buddies' excitement, loudly and finally proclaims his love for D.C.

D.C. steps away from the mess he's made on the bar, slides Slug away and hugs his BFF. Whilst holding his embrace he calmly says, "I know."

The gang of socially awkward morons laugh and point, then in unison shout, "Been done!!"

The two new lovers join in the joke with their friends, clasp one another's hand confidently and make their way out of the pub.

The gang make their way to the side entrance of the market and hide behind some conveniently located bushes. Nash nervously unlocks the door and goes inside, leaving a small stone in the doorway so it won't fully close. Nash is now in the belly of the beast and the others know it's their turn next.

After a few minutes, to let Nash settle in, the first wave make their move. Like clumsy Ninja, Gorey, Sausage and D.C. stumble their way through the door and on toward their positions. A few more minutes go by, and our hero leads his ground troops slowly through the corridors toward full frontal hand to hand combat.

The delicate perv, D.C., gets to his position first, the cleaners' storage cupboard right next to the function room. Close enough for his Bluetooth connection to Gorey' speakers, that he is placing just above D.C. in the old wooden rafters. He can hear the cackles of the elusive market leader as he nestles himself behind the new mops and a stack of bin bags. He quivers with nervous fear. The stress is mounting on the Noughties nerd and he knows if he stays focused and fulfils his role he will need to knock one out in speedy time.

D.C. masturbates.

He's worried it could be the last time!

As he makes sweet, fast love to himself, the tickles from the brand-new mop heads seemingly floating above him help him to relax for those precious moments.

Then the message comes through from Gorey on his phone.

"I'm in position. Get the playlist ready, Gx."

D.C. connects his phone to the Bluetooth speakers Gorey has mounted in the rafters above the demonic beasts and he sends the text back: "All set."

Meanwhile, Sausage has clambered his way into the ventilation system. Crawling silently, he finds the air vent right in the centre of the ceiling where the mongrel herd are partying.

He sends a txt to all; "Set."

Now poised, in position and ready to do his task, he begins to feel uncomfortable. A knot in his stomach? Is it just butterflies? But, with the warm air running through the chambers making him sweaty and regretful of munching down that sausage dinner his mother had made for him earlier. His stomach starts to bloat, pulling at the waistband of the ever tightening, stretchy, leggings he's borrowed from his sister. He tries to wiggle himself to a more comfortable position. But the sweat is now pouring off him in panic. Then, A bead of sweat runs down the packed tight crack of his posterior, he can't hold on any longer.

A massive but almost silent flatch protrudes from his haemorrhoid palace, making his sweaty cheeks slap and crack together as if to applaud the foul aroma which it's brought forth. He giggles uncontrollably, but the more he laughs the more ginormous air biscuits are dealt out into the hot, now humid heating system.

The hot air pushes the foul stench through the vents onto the trapped souls below.

As the flatulent aroma hits the demon-possessed managers they're instantly repelled, belly laughing out loud as they grab at their noses and gag into their grabbed t-shirts. They then begin finger pointing at one another as they slug back their marketplace stolen party beers accusing one another of dropping the rotting smell of Sausage fart.

Our hero, now just outside the room, watches this frivolity through the small window in the door. He sends the text to D.C.

"NOW"

As the rare moment of management frivolity continues, our hero and the ground troops wade into the smelly hall. The music comes blasting out. The matching video beams onto the wall and the troops roll out the glitter balls. They roll silently across the floor and reflect those million candles of wonderful light upon the demon fucks!

The light flings its way around the room, bouncing off the tiny mirrored 'light' grenades as they're kicked along in the panic and therefore bringing all the more light-filled mayhem as they do. The troops, right in the thick of it, begin to sing along and bounce up and down as they see their enemies begin to fall to the floor.

The snowflakes cheer and smile smiles as big as can be, as

they begin to witness their fellow humans fight back against the devils that had enslaved them.

The greedy demons quickly lose control of their hosts as they recoil at the snowflake's happiness and the power of the million candle torches.

However, the elusive market leader seems to be fighting back. She casts the snowflakes aside with sweeping ease. Nash rushes to her, reaching into his jeans as he does so. He meets her head on, pulling out his thick, lengthy light he casts the strobing wand across her howling face, pinning her to the corner of the room.

Meanwhile, Nikel falls instantly to his knees in front of Dookie's light. The lonely man consumed by the greedy demon inside surrenders himself in an act of internal turmoil.

Dookie freezes, with his light pointed at the decrepit twat of a man. The powerful light floods his foe's face as he cramps into the foetal position. Nikel releases a trouser fragrance, screams aloud then almost immediately gives anal birth to a hideously deformed and greedy turd demon. It turns to dust in the light-filled room of happiness as soon as it creeps out of his womb-like bowel.

Nikel lays on the floor, whimpering like an injured animal with tears streaming from his eyes and yesterday's lunch oozing from his demon lair.

"Thank you, Dookie. Thank you," he whimpers.

Dookie winks a sly eye at the man and moves on.

One by one the possessed fall to the ground and secrete their demonic hosts. The dusty ashes of the demons mix in with blood and faecal matter splattered around the room.

The gang pauses for a moment, all eyes directed upon the elusive market leader and Nash, still keeping her demon at bay waves them all over as he beckons for help. They turn their lights to her screeching face and skip over to support their buddy. As they do, she slides down the wall into a hunched-up ball and she claws at the walls.

With the whole gang of foot soldiers beaming constant light upon her face, it finally gives in. A large demon beast rips out of her bung hole and flings her limp unconscious body to the side.

The Turd Demon grabs Getlan.

This demon is bigger, faster and withstanding the light. The gang panic and start to back away, leaving Dookie shining his light directly at the eyes of the beast. Then, D.C. runs in, leaving the safety of his cupboard. He gets right up to the demon and places his soft loving hand on the demon's arm. He looks straight at Getlan as if the beast isn't even there.

Clearly now in pain, the man-sized demon slowly releases its grip on Getlan and drops to a knee. Dookie and the gang watch on, all raising their torches to the weakening beast's face. It turns its head and D.C. lets it go.

D.C. embraces Getlan and the demon crumbles to dust at the feet of the crippled market leader.

Gorey and Sausage switch the speakers and projector off, swing down from the rafters and join the gang. Dookie tells the managers to slow down and stop panicking.

"We have painkillers and adult diapers for everyone, so just chill out and try not to get anymore shit on yourselves, ok?" he shouts out.

Dookie then congratulates the gang and embraces little D.C. for his bravery, he knows it's the love inside the young D.C. that has just saved them all from the large Turd Demon.

As Dookie goes to step outside to get some fresh air and contemplate the next move, Nikel begins to shake. Like someone having a seizure or a suffocating fish, he flops around on the floor and spreads his legs wide, screaming in pain. He pushes.

"Something else is coming," he screams out to the gang.

They all rush over to him, Bree grabs one of his legs and Tupps the other. The rest stand fast, lights on full beam and aimed straight through his ripped trousers and boxers onto the gapping great big torn up hole between his hairy cheeks.

He pushes one great big push, dislocating both his hips and screaming like a footballer that was almost tackled as he does. Then something huge slides out of him at splattering speed! It slides across the moist floor! Way too big to be a log or another demon. Some of the gang grab it and start wiping the brown juice from it as it gasps! They recoil in fear as it pulls itself to its knees and breathes massive gasps of air into its lungs.

Dookie tells the gang to raise their lights...

"It's Miguel! He must have been up there for years guys! And my god he doesn't look happy about it!" states Dookie.

The twitching, shit-covered colon-dweller stands to his feet and growls at Dookie. All of a sudden, Lollie pounces at him, flashing her light in his face and jolting from side to side laughing and joking as she does, saying, "Can't catch me little shit man, ooo can't catch me, can't catch me."

Clearly having too much fun, the young Lollie, turns back with a massive smile on her face and beckons the other wallies to join in.

Then, the angry man that has lived on nothing for years, but Nikel's forming stools, throws himself at her. He grips hold of the hipster as he takes her down to the disgusting floor and begins to maul her like a hungry lion. Chewing the flesh from her neck he raises his head as the rest of the gang slide into attack mode, with all their lights upon him, his murderous turd demon finally tries to escape its host.

The small, weakened demon slides from Miguel's cavity like a greasy burger turd on a Sunday morning. It knows it's beat. The gang torch it and rush to the aid of their friend. The wound, so deep, it's too late. A fallen hero, she will always be remembered. The snowflakes pick her body up and carry her outside. All shocked and tearful, they sit themselves down next to her and hug one another.

As they console each other, the freed marketplace management team begin to try and walk and crawl outside. They join the snowflakes in the car park and offer their condolences and gratitude for freeing them from their devilish parasites.

Dookie goes back in and drags the barely conscious elusive market leader outside and goes back in for Nikel. He throws the floor manager over his shoulder and makes his way back to the car park.

IT'S ONLY JUST BEGUN!!!

Dookie and the Snowflakes stand in the car park. They take some deep, long breaths of clean fresh air, clearing their nasal passages of the smelly disgust they have just witnessed. As they do so, the headlights of a vehicle appear at the top of the dark car park.

The large round lights pause at the entrance. The engine revs up as the driver stomps on the pedal again and again.

Nikel lifts his head a little and cries out, "Oh no, I know that sound, I know that sound Dookie! It's Dastardly Di the Dick! It's his bus!"

Just then the engine of the bus is revved up the tyres chirp against the cheap, slick tarmac of the car park. Dastardly Di the Dick and his suited ass lickers thunder their way down the car park. Straight toward the gathered free souls of the management team and the band of heroes amassed by the front door.

Dookie raises his right arm and holds out his torch and using his thumb he flicks the button to on. Shining the light directly in the face of the driver he walks toward the oncoming menace.

The driver begins to swerve left and right to avoid the ever-approaching beam. Finally, the bus swerves to its left and screeches to a halt in front of Dookie and the team.

The suited ass lickers disembark the bus and form a line. They hiss and screech at the once possessed managers who back away into the shrubbery for any kind of cover. Dookie moves to the centre front of the possessed ass lickers and calls his snowflake army to match the enemies' position, right behind him.

"Form the line! Form the line for attack! It's only just begun!"

Dookie screams out.

He adjusts his belly back over his belt and pulls the boxers from his crack.

The young, distraught, snowflakes are pulled to their feet by Gory and Nikel drags himself back inside the marketplace. Just inside, the newly freed man stretches his arm up the wall and gets his bloodied fingers to the control panel. He presses the silent alarm buttons and holds them in for three seconds. He collapses his arm back to the floor, and, spent of energy, loses consciousness.

The snowflakes line up, a pace behind Dookie, all armed with their trusted super lights of a million candles, they recompose themselves. Bree, now holding her fuck buddy's light too and holding back her anger, forces out that all important smile.

Dastardly Di the Dick exits the bus to command his ass lickers. With his trusted axe in hand, he encourages them forward. One of the suited men separates from the licker platoon and stands to the side. He loudly reads out highlights of the terms and conditions of employment at Hellmart:

☆☆☆☆☆☆☆☆☆☆☆☆☆☆

Thou shall not question thy betters

Thou shall not ask for the following.
    More money
    time off
    union support
    respect
    honest annual reports
    freedom from fear at work

Thou shall not complain that customer facing roles are the worst paid jobs in our customer-based business.

Thou shall not complain our customer facing roles don't get the bonus structure of office placed roles from sales from the customers they never interact with.

Thou must understand:
> *respect begins three levels above the market floor workers*
> *you are expendable*
> *your job is not important*

Thou will be required to work in other Hellmarts around Dragon Valley as and when required

The Union works for us

☆☆☆☆☆☆☆☆☆☆☆☆☆

The licker platoon stomp forward down the car park toward the waiting Snowflakes. The lickers hiss and cackle as Dastardly Di the Dick again persuades them forth with his enormous axe from behind.

Suddenly the Popemobile comes bouncing over the curb, through the small wooden fence and slides in between the two forces. Frank the Fucker is in his bulletproof capsule to the rear of the car and Vin Hoisin jumps from the driver's seat and runs to the Snowflake aid.

Frank the Fucker can't believe it. He tries to hex Vin, but Vin just laughs and gives him the finger!

"I've always known you were crooked Frank! I even know it

was you who bumped off the last Pope. I just couldn't prove it!" he shouts.

THE DEVIL IS IN ALL OF YOU

As the Snowflakes, Vin Hoisin and Dookie prepare for the next battle, they notice other people entering the car park. As these randoms enter the dimly lit areas, our team of heroes notice some are fellow staff members at Hellmart. Others are customers, past and present, young, and old. All have come armed with torches of some description!

How can this be? The team look at one another in disbelief as the locals are joining their ranks. Dookie addresses some of them quietly and asks them how they are here. A man speaks out from the back of the group.

"One of your lot has been live broadcasting the whole thing over the net, so I guess we all had the same idea. Help."

Dookie smiles to himself as he remembers, this is what we fight for; our communities, our livelihoods, our friends and loved ones. He takes a deep breath and full of pride he and the team welcome them all as they continue to flood the car park.

Meanwhile... Frank, the possessed Pope, is tempting Gory, the nincompoop, towards him with his favourite sweets (jelly babies) and whispering to him that it will all be o.k. The confused and ridiculously over aged snowflake is easily swayed. He quickly makes his way over to the evil Popemobile, with the sweet taste and squidgy feel of those jelly babies on his mind.

As the dullard reaches the rear of the Popemobile, the tacky and crusty curtain begins to open. Gullible Gorey pokes his head through the opening to find Frank's demon has crawled partially from his Holiness's hole! Its abnormally long arm reaches out, grabs Gory by the throat and with a deadly grip of hatred he squeezes the life from the silly bugger. It holds on to him as its host screams out to the crowd, "The devil is in all of you."

Dookie and the team look over to see what the pretend magic man is banging on about. Then they see the monster's grip, wrapped around their buddy's neck as it was. They run over with their torches raised up against the evil ass-dweller. The demon releases its grip and slips back up inside its favourite hole to escape the light. Frank jumps into the driver's seat and escapes to the rear of Dastardly Di the Dick's troops to celebrate his kill with his evil clan of infected church cronies.

As the staff and town folk form up, ready for battle against the now vastly outnumbered 'leadership', Vin Hoisin asks Dookie for the special old flame torch he gave him on the jet. Dookie points at Gorey. "I gave it to him to hold", he states.

Vin Hoisin slaps himself in the face and sighs. Then, D.C., eyes streaming with tears from the loss of now two of his friends, tells them that Gorey had it stashed in his prison wallet.

The young, emotional snowflake walks over to the twitching corpse of his murdered friend and kneels down beside him. Reaching over, he pulls his buddies black stretchy leggings down to reveal Gorey was a thong wearer. He then pushes his middle finger between the dead man's cheeks, hooks the panty out and stretches it over the left cheek revealing Gorey's hiding place. He reaches inside; a hand, then a forearm deep. He rummages around and pulls out; one remote control, one action man, £12.50 in silver and then... the torch!

D.C., now back to his feet, vigorously shakes and flicks the old wooden torch dry. Then he makes his way back over to Dookie and Vin, and attempts to hand it over to Dookie, but as it smells and still has some corn and hair on it, Dookie insists it's better for Vin to take care of it.

The two sides; good, honest, hardworking (well... working)

people of Dragon Valley and the Demonic, shit eating, money grabbing, power playing, colon dwellers are both ready to fight!

Dastardly Di the Dick has now saddled an Asslicker. Sitting upon his accountants back in a plush, ten-thousand-pound, handmade custom leather saddle, the destroyer of morality orders his troops to wipe his enemy from his site.

The Asslicker Platoon slowly paces forward. As they do so, dastardly Di the Dick's demon becomes engorged. Swelling his 'Dick' costume to around 8' tall.

Frank, looking on from behind, sees his demented, partner of devilish destruction pulsing and swelling himself into a giant 'Dick'. So jealous of Dastardly Di the Dick, he can't help but stretch his little Frank suit in a similar, but all too wrinkly fashion.

The Asslickers attack! The second battle of the night is well under way with beams of light, left hooks, gooly punches and good old-fashioned nipple-gripples all being used by both sides. It's carnage in the car park!

Dookie shouts out for the music to go back on, and the town folk immediately start to party. Some clown has brought a keg and starts giving out biodegradable cups full of moonshine, then from nowhere a burger van rolls up and starts serving bacon cheeseburgers and chips, haloumi burgers and apple slices or good old fashioned hot dogs. All fees to charity. Ahh the 21st century eh?

What a right good fight this is turning into. After freeing one Nun, a Hellmart procurement clerk and a banker from their demonic shit eaters, Dookie stands back for a moment. He watches them roll around in a converged pool of their own excrement and he can't help but feel great about himself. He calls time and makes his way over to the food van for a celebratory double bacon cheeseburger, chips and a nice can of Coke. Proper Coke! None of that sugar free bullshit, this is a party god damn it!!!

After his little snacky snack Dookie takes stock of his troops. Dastardly Di the Dick has broken through the line and is waving his axe around like the total bell-end he is. Many of the staff and town folk are falling at his hand or running in fear. Frank has focused on a tiny little fella, Dunkin. He is chasing him around screaming at him to become his pet, but the feisty little Dunkin isn't having any of it.

Finally, Dookie watches on as Dunkin makes it back to the safety of the Snowflake line, where the power of D.C. and Getlan's love, combined with their two million candles of light, force the evil Pope to retreat. The diminutive Dunkin, still scared and alone, keeps running. He weaves through the legs of the Snowflakes and townsfolk until he sees safety. A cave just for him. He climbs over a dark and stretchy ridge and into the smelly hole. Armed with his tiny torch, two baby bells and a miniature Swiss army knife he knows he's safe for the night. "Ooh, is that corn?" he says to himself. This is a great place.

Dookie runs through the crowd like a gigantic attacking walrus with legs and storms Dastardly Di the Dick! A Superman punch to the side of the bullying, home wrecker's head knocks the money grabbing whore off balance. Dookie follows it up with wide swinging lefts and rights to the weak midsection of the desk dweller. Finally, Dastardly Di the Dick falls to the ground. Townsfolk and Hellmart staff surround him, flashing their lights upon the fallen cock.

Frank comes charging in to save his demented demon buddy! The old, wrinkly, grey haired, decrepit, pervert is at full speed in his little leather sandals and flowing white dress thing, when Tupps whips his phone out and using its pop socket bungee attachment, he flings it around the legs of the possessed magic man. The old git falls, face first into the groin of Dastardly Di the Dick. Now both the leaders have fallen.

Down but not out, yet under constant light attack, the two demons battle with their hosts. The lights of the righteous keep the two Leader demons contained. But still within their hosts. The snowflakes' lights have reduced the swollen bell ends back to normal size. Di the Dastardly Dick is on his back with his knees in his chest trying to pass the stool of a demon when the army of Cronies and Suited ass lickers pile in. Over the top of the cheering and laughing army of morality and goodness they go.

The devilish foot soldiers commit themselves over the top of the decent people and into their lights in an attempt to save their leaders. However, those possessed thickos just start pooping out their demon infection and begin to neutralize themselves in the lights of the happy. The stench quickly becomes unbearable as dozens are piled upon each other, screaming out in pain as they're freed from their captors. The anal leakage dribbling over one another is too much to bear. Then, the screams turn to vomiting... Absolute carnage! But all the brown anal juice and puke is blocking the light from getting to the leaders at the bottom of the pile of idiots.

Seeing the pile of infected, weak minded Suited ass lickers and Cronies with the two leaders at the stinky, slushy bottom of the pile, Vin Hoisin strikes a match. He lights the old torch and runs in. Speaking in tongues he buries himself into the smelly hoard. Beams of powerful light shine through the gaps and just touch the flesh of Dastardly Di the Dick! As it does, a huge scream bellows from him, so loud everyone stops fighting and shouting and stands still.

Dookie reaches into the dog pile and pulls Dastardly Di the

Dick out by an ankle. He lays still. Even with a dozen or so lights upon him. Then... a small, tight, squeaky flatch echoes from deep within his bowels. He looks up at Dookie, then pushesd a gigantic shit eating demon from his rusty sheriff's badge.

The demon uncurls and raises itself to its knees. The weekend demon is waiting for death. So, from a standing position Dookie drop kicks the foul bastard, planting the base of both feet clean into its face. The beast's skull opens at the back of its head and its tiny little brain shoots out like a spit wad from a belligerent child's biro. The beast is dead. Dastardly Di the Dick lays flat on his back crying. He isn't a danger anymore, so Dookie leaves him there.

Moments later Dookie watches on as his band of heroes grapples at the ass end of Frank. Pulling with all their might at the legs of the powerful demon that has consumed the old man for so long. Vin Hoisin, still speaking in tongues, has his foot on his Pontiff's chest as he shoves the old torch flame between the man's legs. Maybe he singes a pube or two, maybe he doesn't, but the once powerful demon that has consumed our lands with its vile greed and narcissism slides from Frank's wrinkly rectum and howls out for just a second as it crumbles to dust.

The remaining slave demons, weak without their masters' might, all fall from bowels and are immediately dusted into nothing due to the joy and light coming from the town folk, news crews, burger van owners and of course the band of snowflakes that have fought off these demonic corporate and religious devils.

As the battle ends the local police arrive. They apologise for the wait time on the emergency call (from Nikel pushing the buttons), but they had run out of petrol and had to fill out seven forms in triplicate to request the funds from the local government to fill the tanks of the riot vans.

People from the surrounding villages begin to fill the streets, it's like a massive New Year's Eve party with stereos blasting and wollies with glow sticks running around. All the while, our hardened corps of snowflakes tend to the assholes of the former assholes now free to become the men, women, and the assholes they want to be.

Our hero watches on as the few fallen snowflake soldiers are loaded up into ambulances and driven away. As the crew picks Gorey's limp, lifeless body up and flips it over in an attempt to pull his pants up, the diminutive Dunkin drops from his hiding place. As does a set of nun chucks, a tube of Anusol and a 90's Barbie Doll (still in the original box).

The Lilliputian Man doesn't know the fight is over and as he lands on the car park tarmac, he begins to panic. He bawls himself up into the foetal position and begins to cry. Our hero steps towards him and scoops him up. Dunkin rolls onto his back pushing his palms and feet up to the sky and with his eyes closed he begins to kick his legs with all his tiny, tiny might; for he thought the once evil Frank has finally snatched him up to have his devilish way with him.

Once the kicking and screaming has subsided and Dunkin realises he's safe, our hero slips his new buddy into his shirt pocket to keep him safe and warm. Together they watch as Gorey is loaded into the ambulance and driven away. Vin Hoisin falls to his knees, crying into his hands as he too watches his beloved Gorey's sweet little ass be driven away.

As the dead are being dealt with, the Dragon Valley first aiders and ambulance crews take over the car park and go hard to work on all those torn up, bloodied, and battered bum holes. All the Ooooooo's and Aaaahhhh's and general pain filled screaming is captured by most of the world's media in wonderful up-close high-definition footage for all the lands to watch. As the town folk and market staff calm down from the fight they begin to think of tomorrow. A better day. It must be. At least that's what they all say, as they hastily make exclusive deals with one media company or another.

After giving their initial 'on air' debuts to rally the masses of underpaid over abused workers to continue their snowflake rebellion, the team gather themselves back up and go to find Dookie.

The Snowflakes find him with a bunch of the market staff, Surrounding Dastardly Di the Dick as his anus is being treated by one of the first aid crews. He cries out to them in a wimpy, needy voice not to hurt him and that he's sorry, so, so sorry. But the staff and Snowflakes alike don't want to hurt him. They're there to help.

D.C. whips one of his adult diapers from his man bag and hands it to him. The team then reassures him that it will all be ok now, just so long as he doesn't act like a prick anymore. They chuckle away to themselves and the whole team goes and sits on a curb to rest.

As the adrenaline wears off, one by one they all have a good cry. Well, all except Dookie because let's face it, his generation don't fucking cry! Not in public at least. But the bulging vein in his neck does slowly disappear. And as daylight breaks over the horizon, the car park empties of its town folk and Hellmart soldiers and burger vans alike. The news crews hang around waiting to pick up any dirt on anyone and get close up HD shots of the new celebrity snowflakes looking like tired old junkies or malnourished depressed and suicidal idiots, that they can inevitably use to wage a slander campaign on them later that week when sales start to decline.

With their marketplace now free of demonic rule and Pope Frank being flown home with Vin Hoisin (who still has the old flame lit for any of the Popes crew that need to be "free"), Dookie calls time on the Snowflake's rebellion. He wishes them a good weekend and leaves. The snowflakes follow suit.

THE FOLLOW THROUGH

So, what happens at the end of our tale to our bewildered Dragon Valley Hellmart and to our beloved characters? How have their lives changed? Do the snowflakes embrace the new celebrity lives awaiting them? Do the once assholes with newly torn up assholes continue to be assholes or embrace a better way of life?

Dragon Valley:

With the Snowflake assault on Hellmart's ass-dwelling demons over, the corporation has replaced Dastardly Di the Dick with a new boss who instantly lowers everyday shopping prices, gives staff a normal hourly rate of pay combined with increasing working hours across the markets (Hellmart staff will be able to rent or purchase their own homes and vehicles once again). To accomplish most of this the new boss has simply got rid of employment killing tech, like self-scans, no cash tills, the fifteen thousand accountants all on seven figure sums at head office, and has lowered the overall pricing just very slightly to help bring more foot flow back into the markets. The trickledown effect is once again flowing through Dragon Valley.

That's right! I mentioned lower prices twice. Almost like it's an important factor to customers eh!

The politicians, now also free from the colon dwellers, go on of course, to praise themselves on how well they each tried to fight back against their unwanted greedy devils. Unfortunately, they've given themselves and all government employees most of the rest of the year off to recuperate along with a pay raise twelve percent above inflation.

Over the following few weeks after the Hellmart assault, the Snowflakes have helped many other business leaders, staff, local and national politicians become free of their inner asshole demons. As the net closed in on them, the remaining demon assholes began evacuating the bowels of their captives and started to run for the borders.

As the whole of Dragon Valley was freed of the greedy, narcissistic, money grabbing and over all oppressive leaders that had been hoarding 99% of the wealth, the citizens began to enjoy a slightly more honest share of the economy.

Of course, there's always going to be assholes. Dragon Valley still has its fair share of those, but at least, for instance, when they get cut up by a taxi driver, a white van man or stuck behind the ignorant bin lorry guys, they know...

LEST WE FORGET

Our individual Snowflakes, Hipsters and rogue fat bastard continue their friendships and work together from time to time, but mostly as individuals. Following their hearts and dreams as they do so well. Each year on the anniversary of the party of light the gang try to get together and celebrate the lives of their fallen buddies. As time goes on some miss the date here and there and some are added to the list of the fallen.

Gorey: R.I.P
Gorey's funeral was large and emotional. Attended by Frank, Vin, all the remaining snowflakes, Dookie and hundreds of his previous lovers.

Bree: R.I.P
Bree's funeral was a quiet affair. Her family preferred not to have the press etc there, although a large congregation from the Vatican was in attendance at the peripherals.

Lollie: R.I.P
In true rebel fashion her skier type hipster buddies stuck her body on top of a large snowy mountain and then set off charges to cause an avalanche. She will remain lost and frozen in her snowy grave. Well, at least until global warming thaws her out!

Tupps:
Tupps sold his battle story to the women's institute for a large assortment of Tupperware and a free lifetime subscription to 'jam of the month'. He won the Great Valley Bake Off and went on to write 12 bestselling cookery books, all

themed around meals to store in plastic containers. Due to his financial success, he secretly finances most of Dookie's adventures through his secret kitchen project.

Hillbilly:

Jumped on the back of his trusted Goat and left the car park that day and was never really seen again. Some said he died on the mountain climb home, but nobody could really be bothered to go find out. Sometime later Dookie and Getlan spent three months following leads across the globe on another mission but found Getlan on a small island surrounded by Hillbilly's familial descendants. He lived the rest of his days there as the self-proclaimed 'King of Goats'.

Sausage:

He started a tweet war with the Ruskies' President and megalomaniac Poostinks, about being a real veggie eco warrior. He was winning too, until a video emerged of him eating a BBQ'd chicken, washed down with a grilled hotdog and imported beer. Sausage's betrayal of his beliefs were splashed all over the front covers of not just the Dragon Valley newspapers but the world's media too. Sausage hasn't been seen or heard from since Poostinks invited him to dinner to discuss their differences. Dookie is looking into the disappearance.

Getlan:

After one hot steamy week of passion, Getlan and D.C. decided to go their separate ways. Getlan got the taste for taking on monsters, demons, and the like. He teamed up with Dookie and enjoyed freeing small villages and poor towns of the demonic freaks that had fled the riches of Dragon Valley after the 'party of light'.

D.C.:

D.C. embraced the world's media and entertainment industries and became the poster boy for a huge decades long government initiative for rejuvenating Dragon Valley's citizen's moral core. He also gives 'paid for' speeches on the benefits of wearing adult diapers through his private company 'shit anytime'. A judge also 'found' him a therapist to help him manage his ongoing struggles with public masturbation. In later life D.C. became a Member of Parliament, Chair of his political party and then went on to preside over the whole of Dragon Valley as Prime Dragon. He also published a book to share with the world his diaries he'd made during his recovery from addiction, 'public masturbation and me'. This won him a Noble peace prize.

Nikel:

During his lengthy stay in hospital for anal reconstruction, Nikel, called the border patrol on his awful bride and her family and they all got deported. He then sold his house and moved to a remote sunny island to enjoy his retirement. He still misses his mummy.

Dastardly Di the Dick:

Dick lightened up. After months of surgeries and traction, Dick finally went home to discover his family had left him around two years previous, but he hadn't noticed. He donated millions into charities to help recovering assholes assholes. He was of course made a Knight of Dragon Valley by the morally lacking politicians and powers that be.

Pope Frank:

Frank was replaced as Pope, obviously. He spent the remainder of his years in a Chateau where he was encouraged to confess his sins daily, in sittings of no more than an hour at a time, due to the stress the harrowing stories were causing the young priests sent to babysit him.

Dunkin:

The tiny Dunkin now resides in Dookie's shirt pocket. Turns out that the nice little fella has a great tactical mind for warfare. Scared shitless of anything that moves but great on the prep. He has become Dookie's right-hand man in his plight to rebalance justice and civility to the planet.

Dookie:

Dookie went on a few entertainment shows, but the media soon turned on him, claiming his cheese and meat addiction caused him to create more bad gas than a large herd of cattle. He invested the bit of money he did make into a strongman style gym so he could keep his dark thoughts at bay, one huge rep at a time. He is currently recruiting a small tactical unit to carry out a rescue mission for his tortured boy. Find out how it goes in our next instalment: "Dookie & The Fat boys attack".

Part 3

DOOKIE AND THE FAT BOYS ATTACK

After all the time that has passed, the long arduous walk to freedom, the years at Hellmart, the party of light and the global tour of ripping shit eating, money grabbing demons from the asses of the weak willed, our hero sits, sleeping in his favourite, brown leather chair with his Mrs by his side. Both snoring like a pair of fog horns blasting out from a coastal ship.

Dookie rattles out an almighty snorting snore and wakes his better half. She leans over and wallops him across the shoulder.

"Baaaah! You woke me up You noisy sod," she says to him.

He grunts and groans and stretches his arms and legs out, jumps up from his slumber and heads to the kitchen.

"Tea, coffee?" he shouts back.

"Tea," she replies.

He makes her tea and himself a cup of joe and returns to his chair. As he sips at his cup, he tells his wife he dreamed he freed his boy and got him back to Dragon Valley safely. She smiles and swigs her hot tea.

Dookie can't help it. He just can't let that idea go. As he sits in his chair he ponders, did his boy make it? Did he hold on to the light and become a decent man or did he cave into his captor 'Aska Aska'? Dookie looks to his good wife for advice and without him even saying anything she stands up and says, "Well, if you're going to find out, you'll need a fucking army!!"

Dookie smiles and replies, "No love, not for this mission! Muscles Are Required Intelligence Not Essential! that's all I need, not some fucking Army."

The little Dunkin hears this, from Dookie's top pocket, and

immediately gets into planning mode. He jumps from his safe hiding place onto the end table next to where his pal is sitting, breaks out his tablet and lets his contacts know another mission is on the horizon.

He lets them all know this one is personal. He gives them all the low down on the situation with Dookie's boy and the mammoth challenge facing the now old and out of shape Dookie. The years of weightlifting his darkness into light and fighting anus demons have taken their toll on our hero. His Knees don't bend, His neck cracks, His ankles cave under the body weight of the brute above them, not to mention the torn ligaments and muscles and unattended bone fractures from the years of fighting and weightlifting too.

Dunkin digs into recon over the next few weeks, scouring the net for GreenBack Land info. Dookie spends this same time following the diminutive Dunkin's advice. He starts stretching and gets his many little injuries, aches and pains sorted at a physio and goes on a diet!

Tupps makes contact through the usual channels straight away and deposits a large sum of money into the 'adventure account' Dookie uses to fund his missions. He also follows that up with a shipment of pickled goods stored in his new range of long-life plastic containers. Perfect condiments to go with the MREs Dookie will supply for the mission.

Getlan throws his hat in the ring as usual, always up for a fight these days. Vin Hoisin also makes contact to say he will begin his travel to Dragon Valley from the Vatican with immediate effect.

Dunkin's research starts to bear fruit. GreenBack land has now been overthrown. It is now run by an orange GreenBack, the self-proclaimed king of GreenBacks, TumpyTump. Dunkin also delves into all the GreenBack Land sponsored social media platforms like Fakebook, Twatta and Clip Clop to find out what the narcissists and celebrity addicted weirdoes were saying about him, TumpyTump, and most importantly, what kind of filters they're putting on the photos of their deserts. But let's start with a quick rundown of Dunkin.

===

Dunkin;
A little fella. Not much is known about Dunkin due to his small stature; he goes unnoticed for the most part. A tool he has used to his advantage.

Tale of the tape.
Height: 5 inches
Weight: one of those feathers they use to make pillows.
Penis name; Donuts
Skill base; Tactical warfare, rubber band flicking

After being bullied at school for his diminutive nature, Dunkin tried to get work for years but could never been seen during interviews so never gained real employment. Using all the might in his little arms he taught himself how to type and found the 'Darkweb'. There he downloaded plans and pass codes for government buildings, banks and a local toy shop. He now has access to all government records, a small bank account he deposits 0.05% of stollen interest from a multinational arms dealers account and a new ride of car of his choice each year.

He now lives with Dookie as chief of staff and finds comfort in Dookie's top shirt pocket, where he has the ear of his best pal.

===

Dunkin creates a profile of him and forwards it to Dookie:

===

TumpyTump;
This old wacky fella has seen it all. From breakfast in bed to delivered lunch burgers from his favourite golden arches. He's eaten it all. He likes to order kiddy size cheeseburgers and pretend it's the biggest burger you can order, due to his midget hand complex. Before uniting large swathes of less educated and well-off GreenBack clans to conquer a vast majority of the central lands Tumpytump ran a chain of seedy motels and strip joints.

Tale of the tape.
Height: 6'
Weight: very very really really average, no, honest he's the most perfect weight he can be.
Actual weight: 23 Stone, 322lbs
Penis name: Stumps
Colour: Orange
Habits: nose picking and pussy grabbing
Talents: he's always right.
Pet leach: covfefe
Best pal: The megalomaniac Poostinks
Combat: if anyone says he isn't right he publicly flogs them and uses the tears from his tiny crying eyes to burn parts of their skin off. Then sends them a Twatta message to inform them and the world he was right.

Tumpytump can't walk up or down steps, so employs a small group of Ruskie women to travel with him everywhere he goes. They pick him up and carry him up and down any stairs, steps or curbs he encounters. That's all they do for him of course. Nothing else. Nothing. He promises.

He has restarted the war at the old southern front and built a large wall to keep, what he describes as, raping, murdering aliens out.

===

As the days go past Dookie gets a message from Joey in the little town of light where he left most of his old unit of Warriors. The message is simple.

Two hundred booked in.

Dunkin and Dookie can't believe it. Two hundred soldiers in, just like that and Dookie knows, if Joey is putting up two hundred soldiers, they'll be decently trained. The pair beam massive grins for days.

A few Dragon Valley locals offer up their service to assist the mission. One donates satellite phones and radios; another secures a sea crossing on a tanker to the southern lands just below the new border wall.

With all the prep work done and dusted, Vin back in Dragon Valley and Dookie in a little better shape, the small team head off to sea and war!!

THE FESTIVAL OF DOOKIE

A few weeks at sea have given Dunkin the time to help whip the small crew into shape. He and Dookie help get their weapons zeroed in with some clay pigeon shooting off the starboard bow and getting them up to speed with his basic plans.

Dookie spends most of the time aboard the tanker continuing to stretch and limber up. Covered in baby oil every night in hopes of it soaking through into his muscles and ligaments to get him through this ever-approaching battle. He also continues his diet regime under the watchful eye of Dunkin. Not that anyone else on the ship has noticed of course. No, the breakfast time tantrums as he reluctantly spoons oats with honey and fruit into disapproving mouth, the choice of fruit for a snack stormy everyday where he screams things like 'just give me a fucking burger', or the dinner time tears when he begs for cheese all go unnoticed. Honest!

After what feels like eternity for Dookie, Dunkin, and the troops they finally make landfall by way of a small port, run by a distant cousin of a town mayor that Dookie, Dunkin and Getlan had helped free of his and his town's colonic demons. So, no papers are exchanged for the boys or their arsenal upon arrival. Why advertise eh? Dunkin agrees to back down on the diet front and tosses the baby oil away as he understands this is where Dookie takes command for real.

The good port manager is ecstatic to see Dookie and the boys. He tells them how he has followed their years of battles and adventures, reading in the newspapers and Dunkin's blog every week since he was a child. He goes on to tell them about the upcoming bi-annual 'Festival of Dookie' that is to be held that very week in Ciudad Fronteriza, just a few minutes' walk from the border wall, the very place the insurgents are aiming to get to. He then offers the guys the chance to tag along with him and his family to the festival. The guys accept the offer with open arms and Dookie can't wait to see what this festival is really all about.

Upon arrival in Ciudad Fronteriza the team are amazed at the amount of people that are in attendance. Thousands staying in the actual town plus thousands more camping all around, as far as the eye can see. There are massive posters of Dookie everywhere and banners and ticker tape all over the town.

Dookie keeps his head down and advises the others to do the same as the last thing they want to do is cause a scene. They wait for nightfall to get out the truck and pitch their tents. Later in the evening the port manager brings the town's officials to the hiding group. He proudly introduces them and asks that their identity remain 'need to know'. The officials agree and after getting the guys to sign some merchandise, breasts and take a few selfies, they then explain the festival to the Warrior and his crew.

===

The festival details:
The free Southerners party all day and night whilst wearing masks to conceal their identity, so anyone could be Dookie in disguise to the always watching Northern GreenBacks. They will eat hot spicy BBQ food and drink lots of beer. All the urine peed out is collected in troughs throughout the festival. The next morning every one of the party goers will have until nine o'clock to defecate into a brown paper bag. At nine thirty the masses will then carry their Dookie filled bags to the wall and

form a miles long single file line. The collected urine is drained into water balloons, tied and placed in groups of one hundred per wheelbarrow and staged between every fifty or so still masked people. At around eleven o'clock the bags are tossed over the wall. Some revellers like to set their bags alight as they throw them over, it's a personal choice. Once the shit filled bags have splattered on the other side of the wall, the piss bombs follow just for good measure. The whole 'shit storm' culminates in the bi-annual sewage purge. This is performed by the sewage workers of Ciudad Fronteriza by releasing the pressure valve on the works' main flow pipe that exits the towns excrement right over the wall in a fifteen-minute-long display of flying turds.

All this is done to celebrate the freedom Dookie gave to the southerners all those years ago.

=====

The gang rolls around on the floor laughing their tits off for ages. So much in fact that their faces and jaws hurt for most of the night. Dookie thanks the town's leaders for his festival namesake and asks if this could be used as a cover to help get them across the wall.

The leaders look astounded. Turning to face each other and then the good port manager, who's now chuckling away quite merrily.

He turns to Dookie and says, "I thought I'd leave it as a surprise for you dude, but there's loads of tunnels under the wall. I'll take you through the nicest one during the Dookie tossing, tomorrow ok."

Dookie can't believe his luck. He laughs along with the rest of them and thanks the port manager.

"Let's get some chicken on that BBQ then and a beer in my hand guys, I'll do the cooking, if you find me a mask," says a very happy Dookie.

The leaders of the town give him and his team a mask each and Dookie cooks up some chow. The team, the town leadership and the port manager's family all eat too much grub and swill their beverages of choice.

They watch on as the tanked-up revellers are entertained by rock bands, pop acts, dance crews, speeches of freedom and fireworks as the night's festivities finally draw to their end at around three a.m.

The hiding crew awake with full bellies, grumbling for a morning movement. Coffee in hand they join the poop queue at around eight o'clock the next morning. Dookie and Vin spend much of their time in line reminiscing, discussing, and laughing about the varied items that may have made it into a brown Dookie bag that day if their old pal Gorey was still alive. Such things as Tonka trucks, a random flip flop and a Barbie's dream house bring much laughter and happy tears to their eyes.

Vin enters the dump tent first. He's greeted by a small scaffolding frame in place of an actual toilet. A solid toilet seat is bolted on to the frame with a wide opening brown paper bag sat directly under it. A bendy plastic tube comes from the rear of the tent and around the front of the bag. A small funnel is just below the front of the seat to collect the yellow rain that will soak down upon the North side of the border. Next to the makeshift toilet is another that looks very similar. This one has no bag though. A hose pipe and a large funnel under the seat makes it obvious... they're not letting any go to waste! It's a makeshift bidet!

Vin giggles as he fills his bag and washes his ass with the cold water. Trousers up, he collects his bag of goodies and wraps the end of the bag over, sanitises his hands and makes his way over to the breakfast buffet.

The toilet attendant gives the seats a quick wipe and replaces the brown bag with a fresh one then calls for his next shitter. Dookie then makes his way in. Moments later he calls out to the attendant outside, who gingerly pokes his head through the zipped doorway.

"Hey there buddy, I'm gonna need a few more of these bags to get this done properly," states Dookie.

The attendant laughs and tosses him in two more bags, re-zips the tent up and looks to the waiting line and lets them know it's going to be a while.

Dookie, finally empty, finds Vin at the buffet area and places a carrier bag full of Dookie bags on the floor next to him. He goes for a refill at the buffet and waits for the crew to join them. Some six rashers of bacon, five eggs, three pancakes, a breakfast burrito and several mugs of coffee later the crew are all in attendance, shit bags filled, bellies filled.

Breakfast done, the port manager hands the guy's brown bags of crap to some teenagers to set fire to as they toss them over the wall and leads Dookie and the guys toward the tunnel entrance. They merge with the crowds of thousands all headed toward the wall ready for the great big shit show.

Once everyone's at the wall and tussling to get into place it's easy for the small unit to dip out and slide under a fake bush covering the entrance to the tunnel. The port manager instructs them to get to the ladder and then get outside and they will be picked up. He stands guard as they thank him and close the entrance.

The port manager re-joins his family in the line and upon the whistle noise the bags begin to take to the air. All the while Dookie and the team run and then walk, due to a severe lack of cardiovascular fitness, as fast as they can to the other end. It seems to take forever, but eventually they come across an old wooden ladder at the end of the six-mile tunnel.

Dookie makes his way to the top of the ladder and finds a door. Dunkin, being the bravest he's ever been, jumps from Dookie's top pocket and slides down his arm just as Dookie is about to open the door.

"I'll go first boss. Just open the door a crack," he tells Dookie.

Dookie slowly and quietly opens the door just a few inches and Dunkin walks through. He's gone for just seconds when he calls out for the rest to follow on. They step through the door, one by one into the kitchen area of a Taco restaurant! The staff haven't noticed them as they're all youngsters playing on their phones! Who can blame them? They get paid less than people slightly older than them, as if they don't do the same work.

The crew slide out the backdoor into a car park. A great big black S.U.V pulls up next to them and the window rolls down. A lady leans over and says, "Get in dick heads, my brother sent me to meet you."

Turns out, the port manager is a handy fella to know. His sister drives them out of town and pulls over at a rest stop. She tells the guys to leave the truck at the '88' marker at the edge of the mountain range, keys in it. She jumps out and gets into another car and leaves. The guys don't even get a chance to thank her. Getlan slides into her seat and takes over the driving and the crew head for the hills.

A few days pass and the distant mountains come into full view. The boys excitedly countdown the last few markers on the new mountain highway and they pull in at '88' as instructed. Dookie and the boys disembark the S.U.V., all nice and rested.

"Well, that was a damn sight easier than what seemed like a freakin' lifetime of walking I had to do the last time I made that stretch boys!" shouts Dookie, as he stretches his decrepit body out. The crew laugh and joke at him and assure each other the highway was probably their last time but Dookie's just so old he can't remember.

They get their shit together, packs on, rifles slung and into the hills they go.

OLD HORIZON, NEW VIEW

They make their way slowly through the brush and boulders of the lowlands and then into the climbing slopes of the rocky beast Dookie has dreamed of climbing, once again, for years. They climb for days and as they near the top, a man appears from the ridge. A rugged old gnarly looking fella with a big beard and an even bigger gun.

The crew stop about ten metres from him and Dookie steps a few paces more towards the grizzling old timer. The man lowers his weapon and paces toward Dookie with his arms out wide. The two embrace, with big slaps on the back and hold one another for a few seconds.

"Gunner! You hillbilly eco warrior hero, what the fuck? How are you here dude?" asks Dookie.

"Well, I'm good dude, I live out here with my trees and what not. I'm happy. Now Joey brings me by supplies every now and then on the other side of the range. He keeps me in batteries and comms too just in case you know. He called me a while back and said, you would be coming." states Gunner.

He then leads the men off into the wilds of the mountain range.

Eventually they come to a spot that Dookie remembers. He stands and stares at a patch in the forest that looks different to the rest; greener grass and baby trees compared to the stubborn, old, deep-rooted ones surrounding them. He looks at Gunner and places his right hand on his pal's shoulder.

"I'm sorry buddy. I really am." he says quietly.

Gunner smiles through his thick bushy beard.

"That's ok bud. I made good use of those fallen trees in the end. You'll see."

He makes his way through the gap in the woodland to the

river Dookie now remembers like it was yesterday, and the crew follow on. Parked up on the embankment are some large inflatable river rafts, a couple of tents, a BBQ and a cooler full of steaks and beers. The old timer hasn't forgotten anything.

The crew camp out overnight listening to the Gunner's stories of the battle against Aska Aska and how the landscape has changed since Dookie was last there.

The next day they wake at sunrise, load the rafts and spend the next few days making their way downstream. Finally, they stop at a familiar, to Dookie, area and disembark. Gunner walks up the stone shoreline and into the thick trees. The others follow him and find him standing on the porch of a self-built mansion. A mansion house fully concealed by the surrounding nature. They congratulate Gunner on a stunning home and down their packs and fight over the old guy's rocking chair.

"Wow! really. Wow! You really did make use of those trees, didn't you Gunner!?" says Dookie with a grin.

Gunner goes on to tell him how he collected all the naturally felled trees he could and the rafts they had used back in the day to create the basis for his home. Over the years he's added and added to create the eco house of his dreams.

The crew stay for two days with the Gunner to ensure they are rested, bathed, and fed well, and then make their way down the rocky lowlands to the town of light. But as they approach the desert lowlands, Dookie is astounded by what he sees. He stands on what was his previous sniper's perch. What was all desert wasteland is now track housing as far as the eye can see. The dirty little town of light is now a huge colourful beast of a city.

The crew make their way down to the rocky edge of a small road and hide in some bushes. A small party bus pulls up and the doors fold open. Joey jumps from the driver's seat and shouts out for Dookie to show himself. Dookie stands and waves to his buddy. Joey beckons him and his crew over to the bus and welcomes them and his best old pal to, what is now called, 'The City of Games'. He then rushes them on to the bus and drives them to a large, gated bungalow.

The crew disembark and quickly get into the safety of the house. It's Joey's house, where he insists they go shower and change, then they'll catch up. He's placed joggers and t-shirts in the spare rooms for them to change into so they can finally wash their cammies too.

All cleaned up, the crew and Joey sit around his large dining table to catch up and discuss the mission.

Here are some updates on our characters as they've aged and changed over the years - seems appropriate:

===

Joey;

A good guy. A great Warrior. He's spent the past few decades creating and commanding the new 'City Guard'. He puts all recruits through a basic six-week training camp and then buddies each recruit with an experienced Guard to complete another three months training on the job. Each Guard must be proficient in small arms, rifles, bayonet, and hand to hand combat. Nobody fucks with the Guards in the City of Games.

Job: Commander of Guards
Hobbies: boulder throwing
Married with two children. Both are Guards

===

Baron;

Baron is a bit of a loner really. He has friends but can be a little annoying to be around as he's aged. Still as tough as they come and unable to pass up 'roadkill', or as he calls it, 'free lunch', Baron has put down his guns and become more involved in a new wave of 'the all-inclusive church' set up by the new and more understanding Pope.

Job: Nun.

Hobbies: Roadkill grilling. Prayer time

Married: to a mythical being's made-up magic man's imaginary dead son.

Although he loves the clothes and lazy days of being a new age Nun, he has of late, felt like his marriage is all one sided. He has found solace in Sister Mary-Anne who smokes forty a day and has a gambling addiction.

===

Rusty;

Rusty found happiness in his new life helping to build and protect the City of Games. Years on he found fame as the first Drag act to perform in the City's newest Gaming arena. He now manages two dozen acts and is a firm snowflake favourite on his hit T.V. show GGTT! or Gamers Got Talent Too! Gamers come from all over the Freeland's to show off their skills as 'Normals'. Last season's winner was a Gaming Chef. She cooked Pot Noodles, Super Noodles, micro rice with Doritos and her final winning dish was a fabulous cheese toasty. Proof again that Gamers Got Talent Too.

Job: T.V. host, Talent Manager, Commander of the Reserve Guard unit.

Hobbies: expelling his built-up inner rage by shooting his custom AR15 machine gun at rocks.

Family: None. But loves to drag up as a Nun so he can sneak into the Monastery where his best pal lives so they can have coffee twice a week.

===

Joey and Dunkin discuss the merits and pitfalls of, as Joey puts it, cannon fires of fucking hell on to those greedy green sacks of shit, and a more tactile advance from the brain of the wee fella. Once settled on the delicate approach as plan 'A', Joey has an uncomfortable fact he must share with Dookie and the gang.

"So... erm... Dooks, our intel is that your boy is now a General in Aska Aska security forces. And that's a big force, Dooks. She now controls more than just Las Ranchos, she controls the whole area as far as we can tell." Joey states nervously.

"What the fuck!..."

"Well... He better have a good bloody excuse for that shit, or he's grounded!" shouts Dookie.

A short silence is observed by the gang. Then Dunkin asks what his actual job is and where he is. As Joey starts to explain the boy is now the commander of her Northern forces, two Nuns enter the house.

Dookie and his travelling-force pals pause at the large burly and bearded Nuns.

"What up guys, I'm Baron and this is Rusty. Dooks, good to see you. I just got back from visiting our missionaries in Las

Ranchos. They tell me your boy took his five thousand strong force to train in the Northern foothills about fifty miles away. Left about two weeks ago! Did it off the cuff too from what we can make out." Baron states.

Dookie responds, "Well shit, that's right about when we got off the boat really! Can you get me to him? And err nice dress dude."

Baron and Rusty pull the Nuns' gear off to reveal their combat fatigues and advise the others that they "really should try it someday". Rusty has Xris's exact coordinates and offers to try to sneak him into the enemy camp. Dunkin goes ape shit of course. Can't blame him, if he's caught it's mission over and Aska Aska will invade the city and take over the Freeland empire, but come on, there's no need to go ape!

"It's not like I'm going to starve you in the middle of an ocean dude. Just going for a little recon that's all!!" states Dookie as he chuckles away.

Dunkin calms himself down and tries to explain to the aging Warriors that they are all a bunch of fat boys that are going to get caught. Of course, the big-headed fat boys chuckle and tell him to 'shut the fuck up'.

Dookie sets out a new plan:

The sneaky sneak of Dunkin's plan goes forward with the forty strong EGS, Elite Guard Section, Vin and Getlan, setting charges and spy cams all around Las Ranchos and the Aska Aska controlled valley below. Joey will spend this time covertly readying the Artillery cannons on the Drop Off and the remainder of his loyal forces ready to go on the ropes with Baron leading that attack. He and Rusty will go try to figure out what game his boy is playing. Dunkin will set up command at the dinner table where he will use the spy cams to direct the troops and set off charges to slow approaching forces.

That settled, the guys order food in and catch up with one another. They banter back and forth through the evening, swilling beer and munching pizza like they have never been apart. Dookie thanks them for all their efforts and sacrifices and the drunk morons spray him with shaken up cans of golden happiness. All is good between pals.

The next day Dookie slides the black dress and headgear from Baron's Nun uniform over his combat attire and he and Rusty hit the road together like Nuns on the run. They head north to a slim canyon in the cliff face almost directly above where the General should be.

What should've been a slow ten-minute drive before the break of dawn ends up taking an hour because they stop off at an Aunty Wendy drive-through for breakfast burritos, hash browns and a coffee. Once at the canyon they strip the Nuns' get up off and rappel down into the tree line.

They snoop around for a while but after that nice hot breakfast, Dookie's guts are ready to show. He squats and props himself up against a strong, sizable tree with his pants down and begins to fertilize the land. All is going well. A good, sizeable slide means not too much back splatter on the legs, but then the onlooking Rusty's laughs turn to sour face. They've been rumbled by enemy forces!

Rusty, in blind panic, throws his massive AR15 up to challenge the oncoming assault. Dookie reluctantly tightens his balloon knot to cut his birthing load, then quickly shakes the log from his cheeks and wraps his hands around his M3.

Dookie, still pants down, shouts out, "We come with word for your General, show yourselves. Weapons low. Or we *will* open fire god damn it."

An M.G. shuffles out from behind a tree about twenty metres away, his weapon held muzzle down by the rifle's butt in one hand. Dookie lowers his weapon and pulls his pants up.

"Take us to your General," Rusty commands.

The M.G., Money Grabber, instructs them to follow him. Moments later the two walk straight into the General's headquarter area. Surrounded by thousands of enemy fighters. The M.G. asks them to stand in the centre of the makeshift compound. They stand in front of a massive beige tent, waiting, while the M.G. steps inside to report his find.

RETURN TO LAS RANCHOS

The two old timers stand waiting. Dookie, hopeful to see his boy, has a million scenarios going around in his head. Will he remember him, hate him, love him, shoot him? The tension grows in just the few seconds they're stood there. Then, the flaps on the tent are pulled open by the attending guards and a man walks through the centre point and into the light.

"Dad!" the man says with a massive smile and goes on, "I've been waiting for you."

The old Warrior fails in his attempt to stop the tears streaming down his face. Unable to speak, he simply steps forward and wraps his arms around his boy. They stand embraced for a minute or so before slowly backing up a little and both wiping their eyes. The General turns slightly back toward his tent and holds his arm out towards the entrance inviting the two Warriors in.

They all step inside and sit either side of the General's desk. A desk with big fat cigars on. Something Dookie's eye did not miss. His boy takes one out and slides the wooden box over so the Dookie and Rusty can join him in a smoke. Rusty lights up, stands to his feet and proclaims the two of them "need a minute to catch up", and says he's going to go mingle.

The father and son chuckle and begin to pass stories back and forth. Turns out Xris has seen reports of much of Dookie's endeavours over his stolen internet connection his crew hacked from the City of Games. The GreenBacks have the internet, but they filter out most of the free world's sites, media and blogs etc.

Xris goes on to tell his father how he has been manipulating Aska Aska since that day they last saw each other. Making her trust him and bring him into her inner circle, especially after her mother died.

"She was weak. Popping pills and hiding all day. Pussy bitch. I took control of her daily schedule for a few weeks. Meetings, floggings, evictions, more floggings. And I made sure I did it all just the awful way she likes it done."

After that, Ask Aska brought him in like he was her protege. He tells how she told him everything. How she rigs the taxes, scams the shipping companies, and even makes double taxes on medicines. In a short time, the young boy became her right hand and for his twenty-first birthday she publicly proclaimed he could have anything he wanted. He took her Army of the North!!

Dookie listens on as he tells how he has become one with his battle-hardened soldiers. He's earned their trust by battling clans up the coast for trucking passage and oil rights in his short tenure. They now speak freely around and to him, sharing their concerns, family problems and money issues. He tells how he has tried to make the unit as close knit as possible ready for this coming test.

Dookie perks up.

"What test, boy?"

The General replies. "I had word from above the cliff that you had made the journey across the great sea and made it to the new border wall. That's when I summoned my troops here. I knew I could trust my senior teams and many of the men, so last night I knocked the comms out and told the men my plan was to overthrow Aska Aska!"

Dookie almost jumps out of seat.

"What… what happened dude? You're good yeah."

The General flicks the ash from his cigar and replies.

"I had five thousand three hundred M.G.s We now have four

thousand two hundred loyal men and women."

Dookie slaps his hand on the desk with an almighty thud and congratulates his son.

"You must be the good decent man I prayed you would be boy, for all these people to follow you like this. Well done. But what about the ones that aren't loyal to you? What's happened to them?"

Xris replies, "They will stay here. They will not fight for or against us. The brotherhood we share is strong. Once all is done and we have won, we will send for them, and they will be welcomed back. It is only fear of Aska Aska and Tumpytump that holds them back."

The men continue talking for hours and share their plans for the upcoming attack. Xris is impressed with Dunkin's plan as he knows the GreenBack bitch believes she is so powerful that nobody would dare sneak up on her like that. Not that she's gullible or anything, just truly believes in her status and power. He does give Dookie a warning though.

"If I can spend years watching and following your adventures, so can she! And if I can find out you were headed this way, so can she! And if she knows, she will have told Tumpytump! Let's face it dad, if she knows all that, she may very well suspect me too!"

The guys call Rusty back in and get on his encrypted sat phone to see how things are going with Dunkin, Getlan and the gang. All is set in place and the Guards are in hiding at the bottom of the 'drop off' cliff face. Dookie tells of the General's troop situation and that they will begin marching back into Aska Aska's main township within the hour. They'll march throughout the night ready to attack at first light.

The General gives orders to his commanders to assemble the five companies of troops. Full combat gear, bayonets attached, rifles locked and loaded. The men are to leave their main packs and gear at camp and travel light. Helmets on, one MRE in each cargo pocket, two canteens of water, emergency medical pack, six magazines of rounds and one in the clip, two hand grenades and a small flashlight to get them through.

As a Battalion they are broken down into seven companies. Each company has twenty platoons of around thirty troops, each platoon broken into three squads. Each platoon carries one rocket propelled grenade launcher with four shells and two squad automatic weapons with four ammo cases.

The Battalion is also accompanied by three jeeps equipped with top loaded fifty calibre fully automatic belt fed machine guns and two five tonne trucks loaded with back up ammo. The General has also retrofitted these beasts as battering rams.

This is a well-armed, well organised and well fit Battalion of soldiers. Nothing like the pussy bunch of disorganised M.G.'s Dookie and his crew of Warriors walked through all those years ago. This General has spent the time to train his troops to be as close to the Warriors he remembered his father and his friends being when he was a child.

He has trained them to rely on one another as family and trust in him as a father figure. It's paid off. As soon as the Company Captains rouse their men the soldiers go into top gear. Gear on and assembled in platoons, ready and waiting for more orders.

Dookie and his boy pace down the line of men and women who are ready to lay their lives down in a war the two men are bringing upon them. Dookie splays his arms wide and barks like the Warrior dog he used to be, sounding his willingness and readiness to do battle. Rusty hears the noise of his brother in arms and sounds off from the front of the Battalion with barks of his own. The two old timers bark and grunt as loud as they can, breaking the silence of four thousand plus souls. Then, from a few individuals within the ranks more barks join in. Barks from more Warrior Veterans. Dookie howls out to the ranks.

"THIS MARCH IS A MARCH IN DARKNESS, TOWARD THE LIGHT, TOWARD ALL OF OUR FREEDOM! FIGHT NOT FOR YOUR GENERAL, NOT FOR ME, BUT FOR YOURSELF, YOUR FAMILY AND FOR RIGHT!!!"

The General signals forward march and the Battalion moves on. The pace builds to a quick march and the huge snaking file of soldiers begin to slow jog in unison. The Battalion Sgt. Major slides out from the ranks to relieve the General and his already heavy breathing father. Dookie slows his pace and Xris helps him into one of the jeeps. The General runs along by the side of his men keeping in step and singing the cadence the Sgt Major is bellowing out. The pace is held steady for ten miles before the bellows turn silent and the jog slows to a fast march and then a silent pace for the last mile or two.

They make it to the woody edge of Las Ranchos an hour before dawn. Getlan and a handful of the EGS join them as they rest up, eat some chow, replenish their drinking water from the creek and prepare themselves for war.

The General takes a look at the map Getlan has made notes on in regard to his bomb locations and chats to Dunkin back at HQ for any movement noted on the cameras. Dookie looks on with pride as his son takes command.

The General calls a meeting with his leadership and Dookie's guys.

"Right gentlemen, the company of M.G.s now located here at Las Ranchos may well join our cause. The GreenBack in charge is Colonel Hussain. A mean twat that treats his troops like shit. Take him out and his soldiers will thank us. *I WANT*

CASUALTIES TO A MINIMUM GENTS!"

With that Getlan holds his hand up, as if to say, 'silence please', and gets on the comms to Vin and the EGS fire team still behind enemy lines. He instructs them to converge on the house at Las Ranchos.

"Take Hussain! Alive, if possible, but don't put the M.G.s around him in harm's way to keep him alive."

Vin responds. "Aye aye"

Getlan advises the room to give it ten minutes before ordering their troops forward, such is his faith in his new team in the field.

Some fifteen minutes go by, and the General's forward troops are ready to advance down range. A squelch on the mic. in Getlan's earpiece and he shoots to his feet. He waits again for confirmation the fire team are ok.

"Sir, target acquired. We also have his in-house Command ready to speak to you."

Getlan congratulates them and passes the connection to the General. As soon as the General announces himself, Hussain's men surrender and join his fight. Las Ranchos has fallen without a shot being fired. Hussain is escorted by rope to the cliff top where Baron has a few Guards escort him to their jail house to await trial. Dookie, the General and four thousand plus troops simply walk across the open grasslands seemingly without a care in the world.

As they do so, Baron and Joey both get on the comms to inform them of a large number of vehicles approaching Las Ranchos from the south and the coast areas.

Their advance is finally halted due to Aska Aska's troops front and centre of the main road crossing in front of Las Ranchos. Dookie and the General stand in the middle of the front driveway to the compound, sipping a coffee and smoking another big cigar each.

"Well... I guess she knows we're here dude," Chuckles Dookie.

The General laughs and pinches the comms button on this radio.

"Hey Joey, I assume you know what she looks like, so if and when you see that kidnapping fuckknuckle, you be sure to let some of that cannon power rain down hell on her fat ass right."

Joey retorts enthusiastically, "Well hell yeah bro! And good to finally talk to you sir."

The General's troops set up their fifty-calibre machine gun touting jeeps, interspersed with the squad automatic weapons on higher ground with bi-pods out and Gunners in prone. The rocket launchers are kept back behind buildings with the ammo and first aid truck area for added safety. Snipers and their spotters are sent off, back to the tree lines of the rear and the cliff's edge to seek protective areas from which to take out leadership GreenBacks.

Baron and Joey are prepped and ready to let loose, but as they try to amp-up their troops for battle everyone at the Drop off and below notices large aeroplanes flying over and circling the City of Games. Seven massive old 747s take aim at a large flat area of wasteland just outside the city limits. One by one they land on the desert sands and roll right up to the main highway's edge.

The Comms are a blaze. Aska Aska trying to get info from her spies up top and Dookie and the General thinking the worst. An attack on the city! But as the door from the lead plane opens up and the emergency inflatable slide pops out, a female in stretchy jeans and a sweater appears at the top of the ramp.

Dunkin, watching on through a live, wearable cam on one of

the attending Guards recognises her. He gets straight on to Dookie.

"Dooks, it's your Mrs!! Wait one."

As he continues to watch on, all the aircraft emergency doors are opened, and ordinary people start sliding to terra firma. The little fella recognises more and more people.

"Fuck me, Dooks! Think she's brought everyone we ever helped?! There's about three thousand people here dude!"

Dookie responds. "Hah. Gotta love her! Get 'em all lined up south of Las ranchos on the cliff edge. Armed with rocks, or anything heavy. We'll pin any hardcore enemy into that location, and they can't make it rain on em ya."

Let's meet the Mrs!

===

Dookie's Mrs;

Just a normal person living life. Obviously not anymore! You can't be hitched to the lunacy of Dookie and pretend to be normal. But she does cover it well.

Actual name: Shaz

Age: how fucking rude.

Weight: what, you looking for a slap?

Fight skills: prefers hand to hand combat.

Torture: Self trained in ancient art forms of slow torture. The drip drip water torture, the one hair one pull torture regime and her favourite, the baseball bat to the back of the legs.

Battle readiness: Shaz feels there's nothing she can't accomplish with a swift kick in the shin, clip round the ear or a slap on the back of the head. She reserves the open palm uppercut to the chin for real dilemmas.

Shaz is an easy-going helpful type. In fact, she introduced

Tupps to his wife, the first non-inflatable relationship he had ever had.

===

DO GREENBACKS HAVE BUM HOLES??

With the town now empty of families, both armies ready themselves for war. Aska Aska doesn't want to wait anymore, she screams out to her forward command

"OPEN FIRE!"

With that, the war begins. The General immediately has a wall of lead placed down range from his elevated Fifty Cals and SAWs, the snipers start assassinating her GreenBack Commanders and his foot soldiers hold steady in dead ground so the enemy bullets can't get to them.

Dookie walks the line of foot soldiers. Enemy rounds buzzing just over his head, as tries to encourage them and coral their fear into boiling courage and heroic force. For he knows, the waiting game is the hardest to play. And wait they must.

The General gives orders for Joey to release ordinance to the rear of Aska Aska's forces. And orders the fifties to slow to shorter bursts with longer gaps between firings. He wants the GreenBack forces to advance up the slight gradient and into the Las Ranchos vast estate.

Joey's Cannon batteries begin to fire down on the GreenBacks' Rear Command posts. Aska Aska's rear guard panic under the bombardment and push forward, forgetting to keep their distance with each other as they rush into the back end of her main army troops in hopes of finding cover. This creates a sea of Green and Black enemies for the cannons to aim for.

Watching her Rear Guard disappear in puffs of smoke from above, Aska Aska has no option but to push forward. As she does, the Fifty Cals increase their firing prowess whilst the SAWs continue to punish her forces with relentless anger.

As they move slowly forward the GreenBack bitch orders a volley of rockets to be fired upon the General's jeeps. They take two out and that frees her troops enough to run into closer ground. Dookie orders the surviving SAW gunners to relocate and concentrate all firepower on the west side far edge of her troop line to bottleneck them back toward the centre and cliff edge points.

The battle ranges on with small incremental advances from Aska Aska and her forces that outnumber Dookie and the General's by four to one. As night begins to fall the first of the many enemy troops are finally corralled into place at the bottom of the drop off.

Vin, still behind enemy lines and hiding in a building just a few hundred metres away from the Las Ranchos estate makes radio contact with Dookie.

"Dookie, get your phone out and use the Demon app to view Aska Aska and any of her GreenBacks dude!!"

Dookie does what he says. He points it at one of her Commanders and the app shows almost the same dark demonic colours and references as the ass dwelling morally corrupt demons he's been fighting for years.

"Vin, I see what you're saying dude, real similar footage. I'll get the guys topside to look into our prisoner."

Topside, Dunkin and Shaz have jumped on it. Within minutes they are forcing the deposed Las Ranchos Commander, Hussain, to endure the horrors of a Michael Bublé Christmas album. They save themselves some pain by wearing ear plugs. However, they can see with even just a few, slow, highly interruptible songs in, the GreenBack starting to quiver. His Green begins to glow dark red and by the fifth recorded atrocity on the album he's squatting in the corner, crying like a baby and breast feeding himself.

Hussain farts!

He farts again, loudly. Again, and again. The stench fills his cell and the noise echoes through the corridors of the local jail house. And then.... He pushes a stool through his crusty almost invisible unhappy place, drops the tit from his mouth and shouts out in cramping pain, sliding to the floor into the mess he just made as he does so. Then, pulls on his knees as he tries to spread his legs more and more, the farts keep coming. Shaz removes Dunkins ear protectors and shoves them up her nose.

By the last putrid Christmas 'song' they are all crying. The pain Hussain is in from his belly to his bum hole, the pain Dunkin is enduring with no ear or nose protection and Shaz due to the other two crying. And then, finally… Hussain's balloon knot loosens, and he births an old decrepit ass dweller.

The shit covered demon goes straight for little Dunkin, grabbing at him through the jail doors. But it can't get to the little fella from behind the bars. Shaz reaches into her bag and pulls out Dookie's great big special light of a million candles. She flicks it on and shines it into the cell. The demon disintegrates.

Shaz reaches for the Comms.

"Hi honey, it's me. Yeah, these GreenBacks are basically controlled by the same but really old Ass Demons as the last lot of idiots you had to help, we reckon. We got Hussain's one out. Looked like it was a couple hundred years old to me. It's dead now though. O yeah. I killed it. with a bit of help from Bublé's eighteenth Christmas album. Ya ya. Woohoo."

Dookie smiles and replies.

"Well done darling. We'll crack out the shit music down here and I'll see you in a bit. Love you."

The General hears the communication from his father's side

and scrambles around to find the tannoy control unit in Hussain's old office. The speakers were updated a few years ago so he can yell at everyone at once over a tannoy in crisp Dolby surround sound. Dookie gets his music app up on his phone and places it next to the microphone.

A cacophony of shit music is blasted out of the speakers; Justin Bieber's *Sorry* and Kylie Minogue's *Spinning Around* head up the upbeat silliness that should at least put a painful fart or two in the Greenback's windpipes.

Dookie smiles at Xris and says,"Well, that should slow the fuckers down some, eh?"

The General spreads the word throughout the troops to sing along and try and have a good time. Between getting shot at or blown up of course! And as the music blasts out, the enemy M.G.s pause and look around, wondering what the hell is going on. Vin takes that opportunity to get back to his own frontline and the world's people ready themselves at the top of the cliff with logs and rocks to drop off as they too sing along with all their might.

TUMPYTUMP AND THE TEMPER TANTRUMS

Everyone's gaze is taken to the sky once again as the dusky darkness is filled with the flashing lights and noise of more aircraft from above. Both sides wait to see if this is reinforcements for their side or the other. As they watch, hundreds of soldiers hurtle towards the ground. Shoots pop open and the failing soldiers begin to glide themselves to the southside of the battle line, identifying themselves as Aska Aska troops.

Even before landing, the incoming soldiers, The Temper Tantrums, break with convention and open fire upon the General's soldiers. With no protection from this heinous assault, the General's men are scattering and falling to the illegal downpouring of ammo. Dookie runs over to the jeep with the Fifty Cal mounted on it, grips the weapon by its double handled triggers, aims skyward and, using both thumbs, depress the paddles. He doesn't even notice he's been shot twice as he sends thousands of rounds up toward the murderous hoard. His assault forces them to pull further south and away from the frontlines. Dozens fall to his repel and a few get tangled in trees and on buildings as they panic in avoidance of his furry.

The airborne attack that never really took off is quelled. Just one enemy fighter has landed on Las Ranchos. Well, landed… He's hung up around five feet from the ground, with his shoot caught on the corner of the main building. Dookie jumps from the jeep and slides his Ka-Bar from its leather sheath as he storms over to the enemy fighter.

"Who the fuck are you?" demands Dookie.

The General and Vin run over too. The General rips bandages from his first aid kit and presses them at Dookie's side that's gushing with blood. As he tries to stem the flow, he calls out for the medics to attend. All the while Vin stands his ground in front of the squirming enemy, pulls another old-fashioned torch from his satchel, and calmly lights it.

"I know who you are! You're TumpyTump. Only you could be that orange." says Vin.

He places the wooden torch on the ground, propped up by a couple of small rocks he's nudged together with his right foot. TumpyTump howls in pain.

"Ooo my bum, my bum!!"

Vin grins, turns his head, and notices Dookie has been taken to the ground by the General waiting on his medical officers' arrival. Vin calmly unsheathes his machete and sticks it into the flame beneath TumpyTump's ass for a short while, then he turns to his old pal, bleeding out on the floor. He drops to a knee and pulls the General's blood-soaked hand away.

"This is gona fuckin' hurt" he whispers to Dookie, then places the red-hot blade on the wound.

Dookie screams out.

"OOWWW! YOU FUCKER! SHIT! FUCK MY ARSE SIDEWAYS!!!"

Vin pulls the blade away and immediately places it on the second wound. Dookie's eyes roll back, and his tense body goes limp. He's unconscious from the pain. Vin and the guys flip the big man over and seal off the exit wounds, field dress them and roll the Elephant Seal-like body of Dookie back over.

They all stand around Dookie waiting for him to come back around. Vin, giggling like a farting toddler, takes the opportunity to point at Dookie's crotch with his right hand, holding out his hot machete, and beckons troops over with his free left hand.

"Look, look, he's wet himself!"

THE BEGINNING OF THE END

The small crowd of soldiers have a chuckle as Dookie comes round from his pain nap.

"Jesus, that hurt! … Shit, I pissed myself." Dookie says, as the guys help him up.

The General nudges his father and points to TumpyTump.

"Looks like his cargo pants would fit you, Dad. Let's cut him down and take 'em. "

With that, the General and Vin pull TumpyTump's hands behind his back and place him in handcuffs. Then they cut the orange, GreenBacks' head honcho down. As they do, Rusty returns from a battle rampage he has been on down at the Eastern side of the front. He too laughs as he helps the pissy wet, grumpy Dookie to steady his feet and turns to the others to inquire as to what's going on. The crew give him the lowdown on Dookie's nap, wet pants, and the dangling TumpyTump.

Vin then holds the flame back a little from the demonic ruler to settle him down a little while Rusty and Xris strip him of his trousers. Dookie drops his pee pee pants and the embarrassed hard man steps into the dry ones.

"Right… Cheers fellas. Let's get this sack of shit topside to Dunkin, is it?" Dookie murmurs.

The guys hand the prisoner of war over to a couple of the General's men and get back to shooting shit.

The General's men and Joey's Cannon crews have continued with the mission of pushing Aska Aska's troops to the cliff face. Now, as her troops are in position, Shaz orders her 'Townsfolk Troops' to release their loads!

Her troops roll boulders and tree trunks over the edge to begin with. Quickly followed by sandbags, bricks and hunks of metal tossed down on to the enemy below. Joey and his fellow Cannon crews simultaneously unleash their fiery hell on to the trapped enemy and the General's men push forward all at once on their bosses bellowing command:

"FORWARD! FORWARD!"

The whole frontline stands and paces forward with confidence into the enemy lines. Dookie, Vin, Rusty and Getlan spearhead the assault into the quivering mess of paid for fuckers.

Within seconds Aska Aska's Commanders sound the general retreat and raised white flags go up across the battlefront.

General Xris pulls a flare from his cargo pants pocket, pops the seal, and raises his right arm to signal for his men to stand down.

The war is won!

Aska Aska' army of M.G.s take a knee and drop their weapons. The enemy commanders try to run, like the bully bitches they are, but with no help from the surrendering troops they all end up at Aska Aska's side.

The General, his top commanders and the Fat boys converge on them. The young general and his Commanders run through the surrendering troops keen to keep eyes on the big bitch. Dookie and the fat boys, older, wiser, and considerably more knackered, jump in a jeep and drive over. Honking the horn to part the M.G.s as they do so.

As they approach, they witness Aska Aska shoving her arms up two of her loyal Commanders' arses. She pulls her arms from the crusty tiny cracks to reveal a canister in each hand. The evil bitch raises her arms above her head and as she glares at the father and son approaching her, she smashes the canisters together with all her might.

A yellow gas billows across the battlefield as she tosses the broken canisters high into the air. General Xris gives the 'gas' symbol with his arms curving in above his head as he turns to ensure his troops are getting their gas masks on.

"You'll never beat me now! The world will suffer my wrath!!" screams the evil bitch.

Xris and Dookie both unholster, raise and fire their nine-millimetre side arms in unison, capping the ugly fuck-knuckle in the head simultaneously. As her smelly corpse hits the floor Vin comes sliding in with his old trusty flame and quickly rips her pants down and without hesitation, plunges the flame into her crusty bum.

With the faint sound of her screaming ass-demon and some ash billowing from the dead bitch's hairy ass crack, Dookie, Vin, and the Fat Boys all know the fight they came for is over and Xris is finally free.

Over the next few weeks Aska Aska's Generals and Commanders are transferred to a secure hospital wing where the authorities will have their demons removed and interrogated. It's proved that Xris is free from any shit eating demon as his kidnapper wanted him 'pure'.

Xris' name is removed from the list of fallen on the edge of town in a ceremony all world leaders attend in his and the fallen's honour.

Unfortunately, honour soon becomes blame as the yellow mist circumventd the globe and torments billions and murders millions. Countries battle to create vaccines and compel their citizens to stay home and wear face masks in an attempt to quell what has become known as, 'The Bitch's Mist'.

The blame soon comes pouring in on Xris and Dookie as the left-wing political establishments around the globe agree that if Dookie had left his son with the evil, kidnapping pedo, none of this would be happening. Of course, they are connected and funded by the evil regimes that Aska Aska traded with who are now not just suffering the Bitch's Mist but also from huge restrictions due to trade embargoes, etc. since her death.

These rogue politicians and evil nations, still controlled by the dark side and its Ass Demon's, take to Snowflake book and other anti-social media to start a war of words against the father and Son, spreading lies and faking accounts in Dookie's name to spread malicious gossip and put fake pictures up for all to see. One picture showed the 350lb Dookie in a string bikini drinking a pint of lager, and these soft sods buy it as a real unedited picture! It makes front page headlines around the world and is splashed all over the TV news channels. Dookie and the fat boys laugh for hours when they see it. Rusty has it made up as a t-shirt and poster gift set for Dookie too, as it's so ridiculous to them. Dookie wouldn't be seen dead drinking a lager! It's Vodka or fuck all for the big man and they know it! But It doesn't take long before the weak-minded left wing, Snowflakes and Hipsters begin to turn the pair into the villains that 'killed the planet'.

Friendly authorities, however, help Dookie and his wife, Xris, the Fat Boys and their families and many of the senior teams that helped fight the Las Ranchos war all hide out in a secure location. Vin is excommunicated from the church and joins them a few weeks later.

All bound together in isolation they vow to fight this. To fight the evil regimes that have made them hated around the world. So, they train. They train the young, the next generation. They train for months and months. They train in hatred, manipulation, and other internet diseases too. Tupps, still loved by everyone of course, secretly keeps them well fed and armed with care packages sent in daily. Cupcakes and

M16s are always on the menu.

They study the news media and the intel Tupps sent them in from his secret kitchen. The world is at war! The Bitch's Mist had changed as it's spread around the world. Different variants are rife until just a few major ones seem to take control. Governments develope vaccines but the left-wing tree huggers stop them from compelling their citizens from taking them so the mist jumps and mutates from one populated area to another. Everyone with half a brain knows it would take all to be vaccinated and a few months travel ban to stop the spread, but the world leaders fear the 'Lockdown' word as they know their political rivals would create merry hell over it and cause a media frenzy.

Dookie and his crew know all too well how hard it is to do the right thing, in this understanding of the world leaders' issues and lack of 'sack' they had, the real deals will have to take it upon themselves to sort this shit out.

Dookie calls a meeting with the crew to go over the problems at hand.

"Right then guys, we're going to have to go 'get some' once again or we'll be stuck in this mess in the middle of nowhere forever."Dookie explains.

He goes on to list the issues at hand:

1.   We gotta stop these fuckers travelling around the world, like their personal endeavours outweigh the common good.

2.   Get everyone off the streets for at least six weeks.

3.   Get Local Governments to spend their easy-earned council tax money on setting up trucks to deliver real essential products to neighbourhoods.

4.   Get the local military involved in number's 2 and 3 as they're getting paid anyways.

5.   Round up all the 'flat earth' morons that refuse to be vaccinated and stick them in a secure area with some farming equipment and forget about them.

6.   Teach the treasury and population it's better to spend a huge amount of tax money once, rather than dragging it out over years and years as it will end up costing more. Lockdown after lockdown, job loss after job loss is folly.

7.   We go after the unrighteous ass hats that fucked us over and twat the shit out of them in front of the world. Get our reps back so we can complete numbers 1 through 6 unless it's been so long that 1 through 6 aren't applicable anymore, in which case let's see how the moronic politicians and news media companies have left the world by that time.

8.   Get other countries to follow suit on the first 6 items on the list, depending on item 7 of course.

9.   Job done. Steaks and burgers all round.

In fact, they all have steaks and burgers all round to get over the rant Dookie has been on about the world still being run by morally corrupt assholes whilst compiling the nine-item list!

After his miniature Burger, little Dunkin gets straight on the comms to Tupps and D.C. to start the ball rolling. Then, one evening, from the 'safety' of their isolation camp, a vengeful Dookie and Xris lead the Fat Boys as they break out.

To be continued in the next instalment.

DOOKIE 2
WORLD WAR 3
THE OMICRONS VS THE ANTIVAXERS VS DOOKIE &
FAT BOYS VS POOSTINKS

L - #0236 - 290923 - C0 - 229/152/9 - PB - DID3714522 .